THE MAKING OF THE *Family*

VALERIE FRETT

Copyright © 2023 Valerie Frett.

All rights reserved. No part of this book may be reproduced, stored, or transmitted by any means—whether auditory, graphic, mechanical, or electronic—without written permission of both publisher and author, except in the case of brief excerpts used in critical articles and reviews. Unauthorized reproduction of any part of this work is illegal and is punishable by law.

ISBN: 979-8-89031-540-3 (sc)
ISBN: 979-8-89031-541-0 (hc)
ISBN: 979-8-89031-542-7 (e)

Library of Congress Control Number: 2018907985

Scripture quotations are taken from the Holy Bible, the King James Version.

Some contents are taken from What Wives Wish Their Husbands Knew about Women by James C. Dobson, copyright 1977. Used by permission of Focus on the Family. All rights reserved. Represented by Tyndale House Publishers, Inc.

Some contents are taken from The Act of Marriage by Tim and Beverly LaHaye. Copyright 1976 by Zondervan. All rights reserved.

Because of the dynamic nature of the Internet, any web addresses or links contained in this book may have changed since publication and may no longer be valid. The views expressed in this work are solely those of the author and do not necessarily reflect the views of the publisher, and the publisher hereby disclaims any responsibility for them.

One Galleria Blvd., Suite 1900, Metairie, LA 70001
(504) 702-6708
1-888-421-2397

To parents

ACKNOWLEDGEMENT

I would like to acknowledge my children Shawnea Frett Ajao, Betteto Shawn Frett, and Sheldon Frett for their constant and continuous emotional and technical support which has enabled me to complete this work.

I would like to acknowledge and thank Mr. Tri Adams of the Ewings Publishers LLC for his invaluable assistance in the professional and technical aspects of this endeavor.

I would like to acknowledge and thank the graphic design department of The Ewings Publishers LLC for their excellent work in designing the book cover. I appreciate the piece of advice they gave me and the way they expertly translated my verbal description into the most beautiful picture.

CONTENTS

Introduction ix

Chapter 1   A Marriage Is Made In Heaven 1
Chapter 2   The First Child Is Born 5
Chapter 3   A Second Child Is Born 15
Chapter 4   The Arrival of a Third Child 29
Chapter 5   What Will Become of the Children? 39
Chapter 6   Some Newspaper Commentaries 47
Chapter 7   A Wife Influences the Laws of Her Country 59
Chapter 8   Will The Husband Become a Politician? 65
Chapter 9   A Leading Male Role Model 73
Chapter 10   Some Important Occurrences 79
Chapter 11   The Children Perform 89
Chapter 12   Two Major Milestones Occur 99
Chapter 13   Stephen Is Distraught 109
Chapter 14   Stephen Overcomes 123
Chapter 15   A Family of Adults 133
Chapter 16   A Multimillionaire Is Made 139
Chapter 17   Is It Possible to Save the Marriage? 151

Conclusion: Things I Wish My Book To Do 157
About the Author 159

INTRODUCTION

This Novel is Fiction. Although it is based on a real life story, the characters and events are the creation of the author and are not a true identity of any person or situation. However, writing this story provides an archive where specific nonfictional newspaper article entries, made by the author, can be linked and catalogued as a whole in a single body of work.

It has been a joy for me to write this novel, and I hope that reading it will bring just as much delight to my readers.

Chapter 1

A MARRIAGE IS MADE IN HEAVEN

Jacob and Susan Wells are both graduates of a leading university in the Caribbean. They attended the same university and lived in the same residential hall, where they met in the dining room. Jacob pursued Susan. They would take short walks after dinner and on the weekends, and on Friday nights, Jacob would visit Susan at her dorm room. He always brought a gift of the freshest tropical fruits. They would also play badminton in their spare time. On Sundays, they went to church together. Eventually, they fell in love while they studied for their degrees.

Susan is a beauty. She is five and a half feet tall and weighs 145 pounds. She has long black hair, gentle eyes, and raised squared shoulders. Her complexion is light brown. She is a size twelve and dresses very well. Jacob is quite handsome himself. He is five foot ten and weighs 175 pounds. He has curly black hair, serious eyes, and a slender nose. He has a brown complexion. His ambition is to have his own business and become prime minister of his country. Susan's goals are to be a personal assistant, raise a happy family, and support her husband in his ambitions. They both graduate with bachelor's degrees, Jacob's in science and Susan's in arts.

Upon graduation, Jacob gets a job with the government developing land, and Susan is a secretary in the head office of a national supermarket chain. They live on one of the Caribbean islands, and for two years, they live with their parents while they work and save for the future. Jacob lives with his mother, grandmother, and four siblings. Susan lives in a nearby town with her parents and six siblings. They spend weekends at each other's homes and take many trips together to visit other Caribbean islands. Now the government wants to send Jacob to England for a year to complete a course in town development. Jacob decides to marry Susan and take her with him. On September 18, 1979, they get married in a small chapel in Susan's town, and two days later, they leave for England. Susan is twenty-eight years old and Jacob is thirty.

In England, Susan is unsuccessful in finding a job, so she keeps the home, a small one-bedroom apartment above a small business. When Jacob arrives home from college, he always brings Susan a gift, just as he did when they were on their university campus—fruit, a box of chocolates, a box of shortbread, or some ice cream. He is very creative. When he arrives home, the dining table is set, and dinner is ready. Unfortunately, Susan has to ask him continually not to place his books on top of the already set dining table; rather, he can place them on the sofa.

Now the honeymoon phase is over, and Susan speaks to Jacob angrily. "Why do you continually put your books on the table when you can place them on the sofa instead?" After getting no reply from Jacob, Susan says angrily, "I picked and picked until I picked trash!"

To this, Jacob calmly replies, "You did not choose me. I chose you."

"Thank you for choosing me," Susan says with a smile. She takes the books, as she usually does; places them on the sofa; and invites Jacob to sit down for dinner.

This is their very first quarrel ever since they met, and Susan is happy with how it ends. They finish dinner. After tidying up, she puts in her earbuds and watches television while Jacob studies. Both of them are in the living room, as has been their custom in the evenings since they settled into their home and Jacob started college. On Saturdays, after Jacob gets in his morning studies, they take a walk in the park, take a drive into the country with friends, go shopping for groceries, or just go window-shopping. Then on Sundays, they go to church together.

Life continues peacefully for Jacob and Susan, but Susan is unsuccessful in her efforts to build intimacy in their relationship. Jacob always explains that he is just studying. Sex occurs, but the intimacy that a woman needs is lacking. Susan accepts that Jacob is studying and continues to watch television after dinner with earbuds. Stand-up comedians on the television are very funny, and Susan laughs her head off all evening until bedtime. This continues until March of the following year. Now Jacob has to go out of town to write an exam.

Shortly before he leaves, he says to Susan, "You always want a child. Come, let me give you a little boy."

And Susan goes.

Some six weeks later, the doctor tells them that Susan is pregnant. Susan has a good time being at home and not having to go out to work. Whenever she feels sleepy, she just goes to sleep. One day, in the middle of cooking dinner, a sweet sleepiness comes over her, and she turns off the fires and goes straight to sleep. The next thing she knows, Jacob is shaking her and saying, "Susan, Susan, come and eat. You must be hungry."

Susan isn't hungry. The sleep was so sweet. She awakens and finds that it is night. Everything is dark, dinner is ready, and the table is set. Jacob tells her that he came home and finished cooking the dinner and then grew worried when it became late, and she was still asleep.

They eat. For dessert, they have the shortbread that Jacob has brought her. They tidy the kitchen, and both fall into their usual evening routine of Jacob studying and Susan watching television with earbuds. From then on, when Jacob arrives from college, he places his books on the sofa.

It is near the end of the academic year, and Jacob wants to stay another year in college to obtain a professional certification in the course he is studying. However, the government says he needs to come home because he is needed in the office. With only a few weeks left in England, Jacob spends some time on the weekends discussing things with Susan and outlining the plan he would like to follow on their return home.

Jacob wants to do three things for his mother that Susan has known about from their days of university. He wants to renovate the house his mother built and now lives in, open a drugstore for her so she can work for herself and finish raising his younger siblings, and buy her a new car. He and Susan will live rent-free in the small apartment that his mother has on her property while he remodels the house and establishes the drugstore. He expects his mother will be self-sufficient and in her renovated house by spring of the following year. In another two years, they will have their own business and their own home. Susan agrees. The time comes, and they move back to their Caribbean island.

Chapter 2

THE FIRST CHILD IS BORN

It is July 1980. After a slight face-lift to the apartment and its old furniture, Jacob and Susan are settled in it. Jacob immediately picks up where he left off at his job, and he goes into the office on weekdays from 8:30 a.m. to 4:30 p.m. He works in the government building in the capital, a twenty-minute drive from their apartment. He leaves his office at four thirty, and Susan notices that, by quarter to five, he is home. He takes a direct path to find her wherever she is in the apartment, and he always has his usual gift—tropical fruits, a slice of cake, a fruit pie, ice cream, or some fresh flowers.

Susan is not going to look for a job until after the baby is born. She is at home and sews in the daytime, making beautiful maternity dresses and blouses to match the maternity pants she bought in England. Soon she will need to start wearing them. At the moment, though, her regular clothes still fit. She quits her sewing early, showers, and dresses nicely by four thirty. She waits for Jacob on the little porch at the entrance to the apartment. There are two chairs and a table, and she sets out a jug of fresh fruit juice or lemonade and two glasses. They sit for about half an hour, and Jacob tells her about his day in the capital.

A few weeks pass, and Susan starts to wear her maternity clothes to fit the baby bump that has now started to rise. Jacob wants to take pictures of her every evening, and he takes many of them in the yard.

Meanwhile, in the house, Jacob's grandmother is at home all day. Susan visits her some days, and they talk about her stay in England. Grandmother, as Susan calls her, tells stories about the queen. Grandmother is Adassa's mother. Jacob's mother, Adassa Brown, works far away from home. She passes through the capital and works at the opposite end of the island. She usually arrives home at about four o'clock and goes to bed for a rest before she gets up and makes dinner for her family. She is also a seamstress, and on her days off, she sews, sometimes for strangers. Two of Jacob's sisters are working adults, a younger sister is in primary school, and his only brother is in kindergarten.

By five thirty, everybody is at home, and his siblings are in the yard, just hanging out. Sometimes, Jacob and Susan hang out in the yard too after they eat dinner in their apartment. On one particular evening, Jacob's siblings, Jacob, and Susan are in the yard, and Jacob is taking many pictures. He poses with Susan and asks one of his adult sisters to snap the photo. Jacob stands at Susan's right side. His left hand is around Susan's shoulders, and he is looking down at Susan's tummy with his right hand on her baby bump.

After the picture is taken, Susan turns around and sees Jacob's mother looking through the kitchen window. Her face is distorted, and her eyes look evil. Susan is very shocked. Even if she had tried, she could not have imagined what was to come next.

The following day when Susan comes out at four thirty, she sees Adassa all dressed up and standing by the gate. As soon as Jacob comes off the bus and enters the gate (he has been taking the bus because the car that comes with his managerial position at work has been ordered but has been delayed in arriving on the island) Adassa grabs hold of his left arm and walks him onto the porch.

Jacob sits on the second chair on the porch. Susan is already seated, and there is not room for another chair. So Adassa sits on the bannister and is talking nonstop. She has many tales about events at work and about Jacob's ex-girlfriend, who lives at the opposite end of the island

and works in the same business as Adassa. The ex-girlfriend, Cindy, seems to be Adassa's manager and makes up the work schedule for the team of which Adassa is a member. Adassa seems to be having many unpleasant experiences at the hand of Cindy, and she relates many happenings. The lemonade Susan placed on the porch table is untouched, and Adassa leaves when Jacob tells her he is hungry and wants to go in and eat.

After dinner Jacob is working, as usual, on the first phase of his plans and explaining to Susan what he has accomplished and what steps he is about to take next. Tonight he shows Susan the list of supplies and tells her he is ready to order all the goods for the drugstore. He is going to spend the next two weeks preparing an old unused garage building on the property and building the shelves.

Susan remembers the spectacle of the evening, along with Adassa's evil eyes of the day before and asks Jacob, "Did your mother know that we are expecting?"

"I don't know. I didn't say anything to her," was Jacob's response.

"So why didn't you tell her?" Susan asks.

"I didn't have any reason to," says Jacob.

"She seems to be upset since yesterday when you were taking pictures," says Susan. "Do you think her behavior today was normal?"

"She will be okay. In less than a month, her drugstore will be open, and she will be busy every day."

What Jacob says about his mother's impending busyness makes sense to Susan, so she does not pursue the matter further. After watching a little television, they go to bed.

Today is a new day on God's earth, but not for Adassa it seems. She has gotten all dressed up again and is waiting at the gate. She hangs on to Jacob as soon as he enters and repeats her performance of the day before.

In fact she continues the same routine until the end of the week, and Susan just ignores her. Susan thinks she is deliberately talking about Jacob's ex-girlfriend to try to hurt Susan's feelings. But Susan is not bothered, because Jacob told her all about Cindy before they were married.

It is funny though to Susan that Jacob didn't tell his mother about their pregnancy, as he told his grandmother. But Susan remembers that, shortly after she and Jacob met at university, he told her, "I love my grandmother. My grandmother raised me." And he has never really said much about his mother, except that he worked hard from very young and gave her all the money.

Susan thinks that all she needs to do is to get dressed, take the bus into the capital, and meet Jacob at his office at four thirty. She and Jacob will arrive home together and that will set Adassa straight. On the other hand, she wishes to accomplish her home tasks, and with her growing pregnancy, she needs her rest in the day so that she can be up with Jacob in the night. She decides that she doesn't wish to play that dirty game with Adassa; it seems so low and undignified. She is not even jealous of Jacob's mother, and she is supportive of Jacob in the things he wants to do for his unmarried mother. Moreover, the baby is moving strongly now, and Susan is enjoying her pregnancy.

Friday evening comes, and the materials arrive for the preparation of the old garage into a drugstore. Jacob goes to receive the materials, and Adassa helps him.

It is also Jacob and Susan's first wedding anniversary, and they get all dressed up and go out for a formal dinner and a late movie afterward. When they return, Susan notices that Adassa's light is on, and Adassa is looking through the kitchen window with evil eyes. When they go inside, she tells Jacob that she thinks there will have to be a slight change of plans. They will have to find a place of their own to live. Jacob says paying rent will be a setback. Plus, she shouldn't worry; when his mother gets busy with her drugstore everything will be fine.

The following morning Jacob and Susan are sleeping late and they are shockingly awakened by Adassa's calling at the window, "Jacob, Jacob, get up. It is time to start working."

Susan thinks this is very disrespectful. She tells Jacob he should not go at her bidding, and he should have a talk with her and put a stop to it.

Instead Jacob shouts, "I'm coming." And he jumps out of bed, grabs coffee and toast, and rushes out to her.

The same scene is repeated on Sunday. Susan talks to Jacob again, but to no avail. She starts to feel angry with her husband but has to take control of her peace of mind. So she finds some time in the day and goes for a long walk. When she returns, she takes out her Bible and hymnbook and reads some scripture and sings some of her favorite hymns.

Jacob comes for dinner and she repeats that they need to find a place of their own. Jacob agrees and says he will start looking, but he believes they shouldn't try to move house until after the baby is born. He says it is a pity they will have to buy furniture and pay rent, as it was going to delay their plans for themselves. Susan points out that, in a short time, she will also be working, and they can do anything on both their incomes.

The week passes, and Adassa repeats her audacity the following weekend, with Jacob succumbing to her and Susan feeling disgusted. By the end of the following week, the building is ready, and the goods are delivered for the drugstore. Jacob organizes all his siblings to help him and his mother stock the shelves. In another two weeks, the doors are open without ceremony but with a large sign in the front saying, "Adassa's Drugstore."

Everybody helps to sell in the drugstore, even Susan. It is not busy in the daytime, but it's very busy in the evenings. Grandmother sits by the door of the house and calls Susan if someone comes to the store in the days. Sometimes when Jacob arrives home, he goes straight to the store and shouts to Susan to bring his dinner.

One particular evening, Adassa is at the door of the drugstore, and Susan is sitting with Grandmother at the door of the house. Now the store is between the house and the apartment and the door of the store faces the gate, while the door of the house and the front of the apartment face each other.

Jacob arrives and greets everyone and turns to Susan and says, "Will you bring me my dinner, love?"

To this, Adassa seems very surprised and disappointed.

"Did you think you could walk down the aisle with him?" was Grandmother's retort. "Go and tend to your store."

Meanwhile, Susan has entered her third trimester of pregnancy. The doctor tells her that everything looks good, and the baby is fine, with a strong heartbeat. She is now sewing the baby's clothes in the days. Still, she finds time to visit and chat with Grandmother, who has been noticing Adassa's behavior. Grandmother has been encouraging her not to get stressed over it, reminding her that her most important consideration at the moment is to reserve her strength and well-being for a safe delivery.

For the next two weeks, when Susan goes to visit Grandmother, Adassa is at home. When she sees Susan, instead of concentrating on her sewing, she starts her monologue. She tells stories of how Jacob, from the age of ten, would do odd jobs to help her to finance the home and feed his younger siblings. She talks of a lover she used to have living with her and how he was unfaithful to her and would carry young women into the apartment and into the bed, in which Susan now sleeps. She recalls that Jacob loved Cindy, but Cindy went with another man for money and gave the money to Jacob, who brought the money to her. And she speaks of many other events and situations from the past that Susan doesn't need to know about. She says that Susan is going to go crazy and go to an asylum on another island, and she and Jacob are going to raise the child. Jacob, she says, cannot afford any more than the one child, and a child doesn't need anything more than some pampers and a few tins of evaporated milk. She is sure that Jacob is going to build her a big house to pay her for the sacrifice she made to send him to school; he will buy her a brand-new car. When her youngest child leaves home, she is going to move in with Jacob.

Susan understands that Adassa has been hurt and she also wants to hurt Susan, so Susan just continues to ignore her.

One day, while Susan is visiting Grandmother, and Adassa is engaged in one of her monologues, Grandmother says to her daughter, "Jacob has a wife now, and you just have to accept that."

"Jacob, never needed no wife. I can do everything for my son and help him to become rich," was Adassa's angry reply.

"He obviously needed a wife because he has taken one," Grandmother responds.

"He's mine! He's mine! I'm the one who birth him, and he's mine," Adassa screams and slams her bedroom door.

From then on, Susan tries to make sure Adassa is not at home before she visits Grandmother. She knows she has heard enough, even too much.

After that day, Adassa starts to have dinner for Jacob when he arrives from work. Although Susan tells him to refuse the dinner and come to the apartment to eat, he tells her he feels badly and doesn't want to hurt his mother's feelings. He adds that he is looking for a place of their own.

Susan is feeling impatient with Jacob now, but she continues to read her Bible, especially the Psalms, and to sing from her hymnbook. She finds that taking a walk helps to bring her peace, and she starts eating at four thirty and leaving for a long walk so as not to experience Adassa and her obscene behavior. Now she finds that, for the well-being of herself and her baby, she needs to ignore both Adassa and Jacob. When she visits Grandmother, Grandmother keeps reminding her that her greatest responsibility at present is to ensure her and her baby's health and have a safe delivery.

One day, Susan comes from her walk and goes into the drugstore to see if Jacob will include her in the conversation. But she is rudely reminded that it is not a conversation, but a monologue. Jacob doesn't acknowledge her presence, and she stands there as if invisible. She hears that Cindy has cut down Adassa's working hours very drastically, which explains why she has been at home so much.

Susan is asleep when Jacob comes to bed. So the next morning, she tries to tell Jacob that his mother is emotionally unwell, which is clear from the things she has been saying and doing. He just insists that everything is going to be fine.

The drugstore is doing very well. Sales in the day are small, but in the evenings, it is very busy. Jacob and Adassa keep it open until midnight. As soon as the store can afford to pay a pharmacist, Jacob plans to open the prescriptions section. His youngest sister, Charlene, says she is going to become a pharmacist. It sounds like good news for the future of the store.

Jacob tells Susan, "Whatever you need take from the cash pan. Nobody can say anything to you. It is your husband's store."

Susan knows that the store is for his mother, but she understands him to mean that he has not yet given it to her. She doesn't understand how he speaks this way to her, yet he allows his mother to have her way with him.

Susan has just discovered that, when they close the store at midnight and she is asleep, Adassa lends Jacob her car, and he goes into the capital. This upsets Susan so much that she cannot find words to express her feelings to Jacob. She realizes that she must remain calm, so she takes longer walks in the evenings. She stops cooking for herself; takes enough money from the cash pan; and walks to the airport, which is a less-than-fifteen-minute drive from her home. She eats dinner there, watches the planes and people come and go, and walks back home and goes to sleep. On Sunday mornings, she takes the bus and goes to Mass in the capital and sings peace into her soul. She has lunch before she takes the bus back home. She expects Jacob to ask her about her activities, but he doesn't, and she doesn't ask him about his. She fears what she may learn, and she cannot afford to upset herself as she gets near to the birth of her baby.

Between going to sleep so early and the progression of her pregnancy, she awakes in the middle of the night and needs a snack. While she is up, she notices that Jacob returns home between 2:00 and 3:00 a.m. Adassa comes out of her house to meet him and follows him into the apartment. Sometimes Susan is still in the kitchen while they sit in her living room, the monologue going. While she makes tea she stares at Jacob, but he doesn't seem to notice her presence. She doesn't listen to what Adassa is saying, lest it is something that will upset her. She just eats and goes back to sleep.

Most mornings now when she wakes, Jacob has had coffee and toast and is leaving for work. When she does wake early, he tells her of his progress with the drugstore. He is completing a new order to stock the store for Christmas. He is ordering toys, cosmetics, housewares, and such a variety of other goods including the usual over-the-counter pharmaceuticals, and ice cream.

THE FIRST CHILD IS BORN

It is December, and many things have happened before Christmas. The goods arrived for the drugstore, and the shelves are fully stocked. The government car arrived, and Jacob now drives to work. Jacob's two younger siblings are on school holidays. Adassa only works two days per week, so Susan only has two days to visit Grandmother. Susan's sister arrives to spend a month and help Susan in her postpartum recovery.

And on the eighteenth day, a baby girl is born to Jacob and Susan. They welcome her with joy and name her Angeline. Susan cares for Angeline in the mornings while her sister does Angeline's laundry and cooks. Her sister helps with Angeline in the afternoons while she rests so she can care for the baby in the nights while her sister sleeps.

Jacob and Adassa open the store Christmas morning until midday and again on Boxing Day until 6:00 p.m., making good sales both days. On these days, when Jacob isn't in the store, he is in his bed except for when he is eating.

Jacob's mother offers to do Jacob's laundry, and Susan is glad for the help. As much as she would like to, she is in no position to refuse. So now the two holidays are over, Adassa comes knocking every morning, holding high in the air on hangers Jacob's work suit for the day.

On New Year's Day, Adassa opens the store from midday until 6:00 p.m. because of the ice cream. Jacob spends all day in bed, while Susan and her sister follow their routine. After dinner, Jacob takes Susan, her sister, and baby Angeline for a drive into the capital and around the island to view the Christmas decorations. This is Susan's first time leaving the apartment since she gave birth, and she thinks it is a very nice way to start the New Year.

The following day, Susan takes Angeline to see Grandmother.

Over the next two weeks, she learns what seems to be bad news for the future of the drugstore. There are always several dolls in the dirt and in the mud. Jacob's sister, Charlene, would take a new doll from the store every day, play with it, and leave it in the yard overnight. His older sisters would take new cosmetics every morning to get ready for work, because the items they took the day before would be broken and on the floor. Adassa would take a new tape measure and needles every morning to do her sewing because she was unable to find the ones she used the day before. It is not that Susan thinks they shouldn't have a few items from the store, but it is their irresponsibility that is bad for the business. Susan talks to Jacob about this, and he says nothing.

It is time for Susan's sister to leave, and Susan, after a whole month, still feels weak and unable to cope on her own. In addition, she misses her parents and siblings, whom she has not seen in over a year. She knows that, at her parents' home, she would have plenty of help with Angeline, and she could get plenty of rest. She talks to Jacob about going home with her sister for three weeks, and he agrees. So at the end of January, he sees Susan and Angeline and Susan's sister off at the train station.

While at her parents' home, Susan discovers that the local college is offering a six-month intensive personal assistant's course for persons with a bachelor's degree. The course will run from the first of March until the end of August. This is very attractive to Susan, and her father is willing to pay the cost.

Susan thinks carefully about the matter. Adassa will be happy with her absence. Seven months is a long time to leave your husband by himself. A wife cannot watch her husband to make him do the right thing. This is a golden opportunity, and her ambition is to become a personal assistant and work with Jacob when he has his business up and running. At her parent's home there is a helper to take care of Angeline during the day, and she will have much help in the night when she studies.

The situation is almost perfect, and during their next conversation, she talks with Jacob about it. He says it will be difficult, but it will give him the opportunity to work very hard on his mother's house and finish it before she returns. He can have an apartment ready and furnished by the time she arrives. He will miss her, but he will come to visit her.

Everything is all set, and Susan applies for and is accepted into the course.

Chapter 3

A SECOND CHILD IS BORN

Susan arrives home with Angeline one week before her second wedding anniversary as a Certified Personal Assistant. Jacob picks them up at the train station and takes them to their own apartment, a five-minute driver east from his mother's home and closer to the airport. Susan fears it is still too close to Adassa, but she understands it could not be helped. She wanted Jacob to find a place in the capital. But, as he explained, this is the community in which he grew up and is known, and this is where he will have to launch his political career. He plans to run for a seat in government as the representative of the community, and so he needs to live there.

Susan thinks that at least they are in their own place, so Adassa cannot be a problem anymore. She plans to put her efforts into building a closer and more intimate relationship with Jacob and establishing a happy home while she advances her career in preparation to work with her husband. The furniture in the apartment is quite beautiful, and Susan commends Jacob for his choices. He explains that his mother insisted on helping him shop for furniture, but she was choosing some really cheap and ugly pieces.

The attendant in the store said to him, "Mr. Wells, a man of your standing in the community cannot put that furniture in his home. Let me show you some fine pieces we have that will be appropriate." What Susan sees is what the attendant suggested.

Jacob took two weeks of vacation. He spent the first week resting and preparing the apartment for Susan and Angeline's arrival.

There are two bedrooms, one for the adults and the other for the baby. Both are fully furnished. There is even a high chair among the dining room furniture. The kitchen and laundry room are not furnished, but the kitchen is stocked with groceries. On the counter is an old two-burner hotplate, and there is a small, old, painted-over-in-white refrigerator that is stocked. Susan feels a surge of love and appreciation and sympathy for her husband, thinking that he did so much and that he could not afford the kitchen appliances at the same time.

For the next five days, she prepares simple meals in her kitchen. On Thursday of the following week her little family leaves, by way of the airport, for Puerto Rico. There they will spend their anniversary and shop for the trimmings for their apartment—curtains, linen, pillows, and so forth.

On the day of their arrival in Puerto Rico, Jacob has a long meeting with a business associate while Susan tends to Angeline in a large conference room. After the meeting, Jacob and family, along with the associate, have an early dinner at their hotel, after which Jacob and family relax, watching television and eating snacks for the rest of the evening until bedtime.

The following day is spent shopping.

The next day, Saturday, is Jacob and Susan's anniversary. Jacob sleeps late while Susan goes for breakfast with Angeline in the hotel dining room and then relaxes with Angeline on their room balcony. They have a garden view, and Susan enjoys the colors of the beautiful flowers. At midday, the family goes out for lunch and a little sightseeing.

Jacob has arranged for a babysitter, and in the evening, they get dressed up and go out for dinner. Susan looks at Jacob across the table and thinks how much she loves and appreciates him. He is a good provider for his family, and she admires how he furnished the apartment, complete with high chair for Angeline. She tells him of her thoughts, and he blushes. Instead of telling her how he feels about her, he starts telling her about his meeting two days earlier and all about his plans to establish a construction company. Susan listens to her husband but resolves that she is going to invest some planning and work into the building of intimacy in their relationship. All the circumstances so far have been working against them. Now, though, in the privacy of their own home, things will be very different.

The weekend ends, and the Wells family go back to their apartment. Jacob will go to work in the morning, so Susan checks the clothes closet and sees that he has two working suits hanging there.

The following morning, while in the kitchen, she is still savoring the weekend and the precious family time when she hears Adassa's voice calling, "Jacob, Jacob." Through the living room window, she sees Adassa coming toward her living room door with a working suit for Jacob held high in the air on hangers. Jacob comes out to her and collects his clothes at the door.

Over breakfast Susan tells Jacob that he needs to go and collect all his clothes from his mother's house, but to no avail. The same drama plays out over four days. Susan begins to think that Jacob is afraid of his mother. So, on the fourth day, she takes a taxi with Angeline and walks into Adassa's house. Adassa comes to greet Angeline, but the baby turns away from her. Angeline doesn't know her. Susan just tells Adassa her mission and walks into the house and gathers all of Jacob's clothes she can find. Afterward, she finds Grandmother and spends a little time for Grandmother to get acquainted with Angeline. From then on, she will go once a week with Jacob into the capital to do her laundry at a Laundromat. She will continue to wash Angeline's clothes by hand at home.

Adassa's home looks very beautiful and new. The old house is converted into two two-bedroom apartments, and a brand-new three-bedroom, two-bathroom apartment is built upstairs. The upstairs is vacant, and the family occupies the two apartments downstairs. Susan could hardly find her way around, but she has managed to accomplish her mission and to find Grandmother in one of the apartments downstairs. The drugstore looks a little run-down and dirty, and Susan is not surprised.

In the evening, she tells Jacob about her adventure of the day and asks him about the upstairs and the drugstore. He explains that the upstairs is complete, and he is going to furnish and lease it and use some of the rent he collects to pay for his rent for their apartment. As for the drugstore, he has been trying to show his mother how to prepare the order sheets for the different companies for the goods they need. But she is not applying herself, and she is not learning how to run the store. None of his older sisters is interested in learning either, and he is too busy to run the business. That was not his plan.

He proceeds to bring Susan up to date on his plans and progress. He is about to register his construction company and to prepare an estimate to build a house east of where they live. Before Christmas, he needs to furnish and lease the upstairs and restock the drugstore. There is a big two-month sale at a furniture store in Puerto Rico; at month's end, he wants to go and purchase the refrigerator, stove, washer, and dryer for their apartment, as well as furniture for the upstairs.

Susan is anxious to get a job now that she can help. They agree to put Angeline in day care so Susan can prepare herself for work and look for a job.

Jacob spends his evenings at home with his foreman, preparing the estimate for the house to be built, and he gets the job—the first one for his construction company.

Meanwhile, Adassa keeps coming to their bedroom window, many mornings at five and six o'clock calling Jacob, and he gets out of bed and goes with her and then returns and gets ready for work. So Susan hardly has any personal time with her husband. She thinks that Adassa only wants to communicate to Jacob that she cannot manage without him and to disturb any peace and happiness for her. She just ignores Adassa and keeps telling Jacob that he needs to sit his mother down; he must put her in her rightful place and put a stop to her infantile behavior. Jacob doesn't respond, and his mother continues to disturb their home. Susan feels very impatient with him, but she concentrates on her own responsibilities to her home and family and on looking for a job.

In no time, Christmas comes. The upstairs is rented. And the drugstore looks brand-new because Jacob went there himself and supervised its cleaning and restocking. Susan has a job in the capital as personal assistant to the director of an oil company with gas stations throughout the Caribbean. Her and Jacob's two-bedroom apartment is fully furnished and decorated, and Jacob has started laying the foundation for the house he is about to build. Angeline is a walking, one-year-old girl, and Jacob has bought her many toys, with which she often plays by herself. Jacob even bought a Christmas tree and decorations and told Susan to put it up for Angeline to enjoy.

He sleeps all Christmas Day and is obviously tired. So Susan, who is also a little tired, doesn't say anything about going to church. After a late breakfast, she and Angeline open their presents, and Susan has a difficult job preventing Angeline from opening Jacob's presents also. As the day, so quiet and peaceful, wears on and she goes in frequently to see Jacob fast asleep, Susan has many disturbing thoughts. Jacob is a hard worker. He is so busy and has so much responsibility. Susan feels sad that he doesn't take time out to enjoy some of the life he is creating. He doesn't just sit around sometimes in the living room and spend time playing with his daughter and enjoying some of the tricks she is sometimes up to. He doesn't seek time out to spend with her and show interest in lovemaking and intimacy. Sex just occurs from time to time, mostly when she insists. She sets him a bubble bath and he doesn't take it. His hands and feet are so dry and rough and when she tries to rub lotion on his hands or give him a pedicure he refuses to allow her. Once when she thought the opportunity was right, she tried to suggest ways in which they could add some spice to their marriage, and he said angrily to her, "You have your problems and I have mine." She felt rejected and abandoned.

Susan wonders what his problems are. She wonders if he is troubled by his mother's behavior and feels afraid to confront her and if he is aware of his mother and siblings' lack of responsibility and feels disgusted by it. She feels sad that his mother and siblings don't show any care and sympathy for him and don't even try to help him with the burden. Grandmother is the only person in that household who seems to have a heart.

Jacob obviously wants a family of his own. He planned it all out to provide financially for his mother and her children so he could leave them. But financial support doesn't seem enough for Adassa. She wants the man. She wants Jacob to be her surrogate spouse and forever support her home and raise her children, just as he has been doing from the age of ten. She has no plan for him to have a life of his own. Moreover, she is jealous of another woman by his side. She actually thinks that place is hers, and Susan thinks that is child abuse. She wonders if Jacob is tired of his surrogate spouse responsibilities and feels trapped, but of course he doesn't share his deeper thoughts with her.

Christmas evening after dinner and after much reminding from Susan, Jacob opens his presents. Shortly afterward, he has a meeting at home with his foreman. He eats breakfast and sleeps all Boxing Day until dinner. Then he brings Grandmother for a short visit to eat ice cream and fruitcake Susan has made for the holidays. He takes the family and Grandmother for a long drive around to see the lights and Christmas decorations.

The next week is work at the office for Jacob. In the evenings, he eats and goes with his foreman to the building he is constructing, and then they return home and study plans until late in the night. Susan's office is closed for the week until the New Year.

On New Year's Day, Jacob sleeps late and then eats breakfast and spends the day with his foreman on the construction site. He says it is necessary preparation to have everything ready for work to begin full scale the following day.

From then on, the procedure is that Susan works five days in her office with Angeline in day care. Jacob works seven days per week, five of the days in his office, and evenings on construction. On the weekends, he works days on his construction business and spends the evenings sleeping. He has to rise early every morning to take water and ice to the construction site for the workmen. On Saturdays and Sundays, Susan prepares a cooked lunch for Jacob and his foreman because the construction site is very close to their apartment.

This lifestyle begins to take its toll on Susan's emotions. The only time she spends with Jacob is on the morning and evening drive to and from work, and when she tries to speak with him, his mind is distant. She feels isolated and has no adult contact and communication. The few female friends she tries to reach out to are busy with their own work and family, and they don't have time just to chat on the phone.

Apart from all this, Susan is concerned about her husband's well-being, their marriage, and the quality of their family life. Family has been a topic of interest to Susan from very young, and she remembers winning an essay competition in her early high school years on the topic of the family. She would read anything she came across about family life, and she sought out and read many books about marriage, family relationships, and roles and responsibilities of family members. She thinks highly of marriage and family and wants to be the maker of a happy family.

She suggests to Jacob that he work six days per week and take Sundays off to rest, thank and worship God, and have family activities. He doesn't comply. So she suggests just taking off Sunday afternoons. When he doesn't honor her request, she suggests one Sunday per month and then one Sunday afternoon per month and is unsuccessful.

She begins to feel unloved and rejected and to see Jacob as impossible to work with. She ceases pursuing him and puts all her efforts into finding her own peace and making Angeline happy. She takes the bus with Angeline on Sunday mornings and goes to Mass in the capital. She keeps her home clean and comfortable and enjoys Angeline and her work. It is tiring, and when Jacob comes in and makes a mess, she gets angry with him because it upsets and destabilizes the peace and comfort of the home.

Meanwhile, during all this, Susan is dealing with her second pregnancy. When Angeline turned one year old, she felt she was ready for her second child. She felt unsure of the direction their marriage was taking, and she was sure she wanted a family. So with that in mind, she did her calculations and seduced Jacob when the time was right.

Some six weeks later her doctor confirmed that she was pregnant. She decided not to tell Jacob but to let him discover it himself. Now she is at the end of her second trimester and enjoying her pregnancy. Apart from a little nausea at the beginning, she has had really enjoyable pregnancies. It is a time when she feels a great sense of well-being, and she experiences the joy and pleasure of having a new life inside her. Both her and baby are well, and Angeline is excited. The only thing she lacks is an affectionate husband who is just as excited to share the joy and pleasure.

Jacob didn't notice her growing baby bump until she started wearing maternity clothes, and he said to her, "Why didn't you tell me you were pregnant?"

"Because you were too busy," was her reply.

"But that's important," he said.

"So all the other things I try to talk with you about are not important then?"

There was no reply.

Now every so often in the mornings when she gets into the car, he asks her how she is feeling, and she responds, "Well," or, "Excited," or, "Unloved," or "Alone."

He inevitably replies, "I am working for us, now all four of us."

And he brings home a new child's bed for the children's room (Angeline has been sleeping in the crib), extra orange juice and fruits in the groceries, and flowers for the dining table.

When Adassa observed that Susan was pregnant she was livid. She told Susan's neighbor, who works at the same place as her, that Susan wants to bankrupt Jacob, and she wishes that the baby would choke her to death. Meanwhile, Susan sees her driving a brand-new car and realizes that Jacob has accomplished his entire plan for his mother. She feels pleased for Jacob, thinking he has earned his freedom.

All these months she has been working, Jacob has never asked her about her salary. He has not discussed any finances with her, and he has not asked her to contribute financially to the home. He does not allow any material thing to be needed in the home. In fact, he has told her that he plans to get a helper before the baby is born; he has started to bring individuals for her to interview. He says he is too busy to help around the house, and a helper will clean up behind him so Susan will not have to get angry with the mess he makes.

She is already angry with him because he has been staying out late at nights and coming home at two and three o'clock again. She does not accept his excuse that he has to work. Now that the house he was building is finished and has been recently handed over, he has been talking to her after dinner about his next project. But when she goes to sleep, he leaves home, and when she awakes in the middle of the night, he is not there. She is just alone with baby Angeline. For the sake of her well-being and the baby's, she tries to think that he is really working on the drawing plans for his next project. He is going to build for himself a restaurant and bar and nightclub. He has bought a piece of prime commercial land right by the water's edge, where he plans to build, in phases, a marina. He is doing very well financially, and Susan is pleased with what he has accomplished in less than two years.

The only project that has a mortgage is his mother's house, and between the income from the drugstore and the upstairs, that mortgage is covered. The drugstore is such a lucrative business (it was well needed in the community) that, if it were run properly, his mother could support her home and have savings from its proceeds. However, on the contrary, the store simply operates on a cycle of run down and build up. When it gets all dirty and disorganized and the shelves are looking empty, Jacob has to go there himself to supervise its cleaning, organizing, and restocking. So instead of growing and expanding, the drugstore is stagnant.

Susan considers that God has blessed Jacob's hands and everything to which he puts them. God causes him to prosper. She fears that, without a proper balance of all the aspects of life—work, personal and family values, praise and thanksgiving to God, being frank with his mother and showing her areas where she needs to improve and know her place, and taking a leadership role in the whole affair—he will not be able to sustain success. She thinks he is hiding some personal weaknesses behind work, instead of taking time for himself to grow spiritually and emotionally.

She herself has been seeking answers for her flawed marriage and comfort for her loneliness and pain in the Bible. She does not intend to despair. Although she loves and appreciates her husband, she is finding it difficult to develop a healthy respect for him, and she does not have any opportunity to discuss these issues. Jacob is very insensitive to any need in the home other than physical need, and her emotions are being constantly challenged. Meanwhile, she is intent on meeting the emotional needs of her children (born and unborn). This means she has to be giving out to the children what she is not receiving to replenish her own emotional resources.

It is in light of all this that their second child is born on October 21, 1982. He is a boy, and they call him Nicholas. For the first month of Susan's postpartum, Jacob pays the helper to work on the weekends. After her first two evenings home from the hospital, he relapses into his usual absenteeism. Even when she gets up in the nights to feed Nicholas, she is alone with the two children in the house and feels so lonely.

The only difference is that Jacob now spends Saturdays and Sundays at home—sleeping. He doesn't show special interest in the children except to see that the supplies are in the home to meet their physical needs. Or if Angeline is fussy, he will take her to bed with him to sleep. "Susan begins to feel that he is nothing more than one of the pieces of furniture in their bedroom."

> *"Susan begins to feel that he is nothing more than one of the pieces of furniture in their bedroom."*

She spends three months maternity leave at home, and by the time she is ready to return to work, she and the helper have developed a kind of friendship. The helper, Carol, has shown herself to be trustworthy, responsible, reliable, and dependable, and she is loving toward the children. Susan feels confident leaving them in her care.

As soon as she returns to work, Jacob advises Susan that she needs her own car. She argues that she doesn't want to have a car of her own; the only time she spends with him is on the drive to and from work. He insists that she should have her own car, and in less than a month, he takes her to see a great deal he has found.

She likes the car, and it is a great deal (a six-month-old Mazda 929 that had been returned to the dealer because the owner had suddenly been assigned to an overseas office in his company). It looks brand new inside, under the hood, and outside, and she likes the color. She buys the car in cash; it is the first major item she is required to spend on since she started to work. She drives to work and to church with the children.

Although she tells Carol, the helper, that the children come first when it comes to allocating her time and effort, when Susan arrives home from work, the entire house is clean and tidy; and the children are fresh and clean and have just returned from an evening walk or are still out walking. Carol says that the children are happy and well behaved, and they like to play on their own with their toys. This gives her time to do a lot. There is even a light meal left in the kitchen from whatever Carol had cooked for their lunch. So with Jacob not even bothering to come home for dinner (he goes from one job to the next) Susan has no need to cook. She, therefore, does all the washing on Saturdays.

Carol is a person of high integrity, and she takes interest and pride in the work she does. Susan says she puts her signature to her work. Susan has lost all fear of leaving Carol in the home with Jacob in the mornings. In fact, Carol says that Jacob is a decent man, and she has come to feel comfortable working in the home with him when Susan is not around. She had left her last job because the husband would not stop making sexual advances at her.

Susan believes, however, that Jacob is having an affair. Yes, he is working on phase one of his development, but she does not think that any man would work so hard that he doesn't take time out for sex. He is not showing any interest in her, and she feels sure he has another woman. Susan is so emotionally upset that she cannot put the matter into words. So she becomes quarrelsome and fusses about this and that and everything except what she really wants to say. She and Jacob begin to have frequent quarrels on Saturdays about a variety of trivial matters.

One particular Saturday, the children are taking their midmorning nap, and many troubling thoughts overwhelm Susan. She feels she just must have Jacob's attention. In her heart, she wants to kiss him on the lips and awaken him like she used to do before they were married. But with anger inside her, she can't bring herself to be so intimate. Instead, she starts to hit him lightly with a broomstick. To her surprise, he jumps out of bed and gives her a slap across the head and returns to his bed. This incident brings a new dimension to their relationship and a greater divide between them.

With the children getting so big—Nicholas is one, and Angeline is almost three—Susan spends as much time as she can in the yard with them exploring. As a result, she has grown very close to the neighbor, who also has two small children—a boy who is older than Angeline and a younger boy who is the same age as Angeline and born in the same month exactly one week apart.

Carol baked a cake for Nicholas on the day he celebrated his first birthday, and Susan invited the neighbor's sons to come over and eat ice cream and cake and sing "Happy Birthday."

She and the neighbor, Margret, are planning to have a small birthday party together for Margret's younger son and Angeline and invite a few more children in the neighborhood.

With this closeness, Susan begins to confide in Margret, only to learn that Margret knows a lot about her and her situation. Margret could tell her that Jacob has a woman named Nora Blinkot, a friend of Adassa's who lives and works in the capital as a kitchen help in a small local restaurant where Jacob usually eats his lunch. Blinkot is regularly seen with Adassa, who drives her around, sometimes past their apartment to and from the airport. Blinkot is from another island. Margret says Jacob has been keeping her since 1980; she knows this because it is from that time that Adassa has been talking at work about the relationship. (Margret is the neighbor who works at the same place as Adassa.) Jacob and Nora Blinkot are sometimes together at Adassa's house.

Susan doesn't need to hear anything more. For example, she doesn't need to know what else Adassa has to say on the job, which Margret says is a lot and has everyone upset and the manager, Cindy, wanting to get rid of her.

To have the real name of a real person added to the situation is an entirely different matter. Susan is devastated. She doesn't know the place where the pain is; it is too deep. She spends much time crying and looking in the mirror, wondering if the reflection she sees is really her.

Meanwhile, she remembers that she has to be strong and well for her children (because she feels they are hers; Jacob has never once changed a diaper or administer a feeding). She cannot bring the words *another woman* to her lips, so she cannot bring the subject to Jacob even if she gets the chance. Although she is actually a very peaceful person, quarrels continue to ensue on Saturdays and unpleasant words are exchanged.

Susan keeps Sundays peaceful and continues to go to church with the children and read her Bible for comfort and answers. Being saturated with the Psalms, she now starts to search the Proverbs. On one particular Saturday as she tries to take a shower, she cannot stop herself from crying (in the shower is where she mostly cries, when she has time to herself to think).

Somehow, Angeline finds out she is crying and goes to her father and says, "Daddy, Mommy is crying."

Jacob comes into the bathroom and asks her, "Why are you crying?"

She wonders if he can't think of a thousand things he is doing or not doing that he should be doing that could make her cry. Overwhelmed by the atrocity of her situation and incapable of saying the damnable words *your woman* she just replies, "It's nothing."

Instead of probing or trying to be of comfort, Jacob just walks away. Susan realizes that she is on her own.

By Christmas, she has pulled herself together and learned many things that God has to say about unfaithfulness. What she never gets to understand, however, is what causes Jacob to need another woman while she is at home lonely and in need. She examines herself and continues to examine God's word.

The birthday party for Angeline and the neighbor's son is very successful, and Christmas comes and is celebrated much like the previous one. Susan decorates the house all by herself, and she and the children decorate the Christmas tree, under which Jacob puts many presents for her and the children. There are also several presents for him, which he opens only after much pleading.

Now that the children are walking and Angeline is talking, he interacts with them a little. They get a little attached to him and sleep with him in the daytime when he is home on holidays or on weekends. But as soon as he gets up at about six in the evening, he takes a shower, gets dressed, and leaves home. When the children cry at the door to go with him, he just shuts the door and leaves them there crying. This is heartbreaking for Susan, who has to comfort them and turn their attention to their toys or story time.

The peace and joy of Christmas really fills Susan, and she refrains from unpleasant thoughts and words. Instead, she grasps every opportunity to be pleasant and kind to Jacob. She even starts kneeling at the bedside, putting her hands on his head, and praying for him when he is asleep in the daytime. Her kindnesses do not stimulate any consideration from him, and he just continues in his way of life.

Peace runs so deep within Susan that she even has positive thoughts about Adassa. She thinks that maybe they can have a common project. She decides to approach Adassa and try to solicit her influence on Jacob to get him off the streets. One day in the week between Christmas and New Year when she is off from work (her office closes that week every year), she goes to see Adassa.

After greetings and pleasantries, Susan reaches the point where she says that Jacob is keeping a woman.

Adassa's swift response is, "It ain' nothing. It ain' nothing. It ain' nothing if a man keep woman with his wife. He ain' save. It ain' nothing."

Well, although Susan knew that Adassa had had her five children with four different men, Susan did not judge her. She just appreciated her for having raised a son that she, Susan, could have to marry. She would have told her of her appreciation had she gotten the chance. But this day, Susan is enlightened to the fact that lack of money is not the poverty Jacob's family grew up in; they were poor from deep, deep within, and all his efforts to raise their economic standing would be in vain.

Chapter 4

THE ARRIVAL OF A THIRD CHILD

In spring 1984 the restaurant, bar, and nightclub open. Toward the end, Jacob had the construction going day and night. There was a day crew and a night crew. His foreman supervised the work during the day, and he was the night supervisor. He went to Puerto Rico on several different trips to furnish and stock the entire establishment. For the restaurant, he bought the finest and most beautiful dinnerware and silverware because he envisioned a fine, formal dining restaurant. Now the entire establishment has a refined finish and decoration, because he intends it all to be of a formal and high-class nature. Using his list of speakers, Susan has prepared the program for the ceremony. The weather is just perfect for the occasion because the ceremony is outdoors right in front of the entrance. Several political leaders speak, praising the development of the community and offering congratulations and wishes for prosperity to Jacob. There is a religious leader to offer blessings, and as Jacob asked, Susan cuts the ribbon at the entrance. Adassa is not present because she is off island with one of her younger children. Carol, the helper, has come to the ceremony to tend Angeline and Nicholas.

Following the evening ceremony, refreshments are served and the bar is open for one hour. Then the settings for refreshments are cleared away, and the place is open for business. Jacob has employed professional chefs and fine waitresses for day and night service in the restaurant and professional bartenders for nights. Everyone praises the quality of the place, which they say has long been needed, especially for night entertainment.

The earnings on the first night are phenomenal, and Susan is surprised. The business becomes very popular, and the community is happy to support a local businessman.

The establishment continues to do very well financially, and Susan sees the lunchtime crowd because she eats lunch there. If she is there for lunch and Jacob comes by, he doesn't join her for lunch or talk to her. He just speaks to the staff and leaves. She feels somewhat embarrassed in the presence of the public and staff.

Speaking of embarrassment, it is Susan's constant companion ever since she confirmed Jacob's unfaithfulness. She has to muster up a great deal of courage to go out in public.

At home, her husband is just as indifferent to her as he is in public. His cycle is such that, during the week, she leaves him in bed in the mornings, hears him come in in the early morning hours, and leaves him in bed again when she goes to work next morning. On weekends now, he comes home in the midmorning hours, sleeps until six in the evening, and then leaves and returns next midmorning. Of course she feels like a single woman. And yet she is married.

So she decides to make the best of her situation; to enjoy whatever pleasures she has being married, while also enjoying some pleasures in feeling single. A few times, she has tried to communicate with him since the New Year about why he is treating her in this way. Why does he need a woman on the street? Is there something wrong with her or in the home? But he has nothing to say. She gets Carol to babysit the children a few nights and goes to the nightclub and behind the bar, but she feels lost because she doesn't know anything about the affairs. She desires to put her small children to bed at nights, and the effort doesn't help her and Jacob's relationship; so she stops.

THE ARRIVAL OF A THIRD CHILD

She resigns herself to the condition. Therefore, although she wanted three children, she decides that she will just have to be satisfied with the two she has, especially since Angeline and Nicholas are a pair. She only wants to ensure that the children are raised emotionally well.

She continues to read her Bible, and she is very surprised to see the things that God says in His word about every aspect of life. As she reads, she examines herself and makes changes where necessary to conform to Christlike standards. One change she makes is that she rises a half an hour earlier and makes Jacob's breakfast just the way he likes it and leaves it covered on the table. He doesn't eat it. Carol says that, as soon as he leaves in the mornings, she sits at the table and enjoys the breakfast. Susan continues to put her hands on Jacob's head and pray for him when he is in bed in the daytime, and she prays for her family and decides to trust God to bring about changes.

When the children are asleep at nights, she reads avidly—books on child development, on the marriage relationship, and on better health, as well as different magazines and newspapers. She has many ideas about family life and the way her situation could improve, and she has no one to discuss them with. She realizes that her situation is common to many families, and she has many ideas about how children could be educated and raised to improve the condition. With all the thoughts in her head she develops trouble sleeping. When she is awake at night, she gets out of bed and writes down her thoughts.

Meanwhile, Jacob makes many trips overseas to meet with business associates. Sometimes, he entertains business associates on the island. Some businessmen come with their wives or even their families; they have young families like Jacob's. Jacob has to take them out to dinner, and when he does, he invites Susan. She feels used by him only for appearances, and she feels angry and resentful and has thoughts of refusing to go. However, she realizes dining out in expensive restaurants is one of the benefits of her marriage, and she will not deny herself the pleasure. He treats her just as indifferently in the presence of his associates. Sometimes, the very men he is entertaining offer Susan assistance where Jacob is failing; they may pull her chair or help her when she tries to put on her jacket—that is, when they are without their wives.

From time to time, Susan writes little naughty, sexy notes from at home and sticks them in Jacob's shirt pocket at the table. He reads them expressionless at the table, and then when they get home, he shows a little interest in her body. No discussion, no saying how he thinks or feels, and then he just returns to his regular lifestyle.

In spite of all this, they have few arguments – only the occasional small spat in which no problems are solved.

You would have thought that you heard the last of Adassa. Well, it was sometime in the summer that same year that Susan begins to notice, whenever she goes for lunch, that Adassa is in the restaurant kitchen. What has happened is that Adassa has left her drugstore and has gone to be the head of the new business. She claims to be a chef in the daytime, and at nights she is bartender. Maybe she doesn't know the job of a night chef, or she is proficient in many trades. This is the point at which Susan thinks Jacob should have sat his mother down and explained to her that he established the drugstore for her, and she need to go take care of it, run it, and support herself.

Jacob doesn't do that, and Susan starts to think he may be afraid of his mother. He does have a scar on his face where he says she hit him with a large spoon when he was young, but he takes all the blame for it.

In no time, Adassa has all the staff tormented with her supervision. The day chef leaves first and then gradually the waitresses. The night staff in the restaurant manages to work through the Christmas busy time. They, too, eventually leave, so the restaurant begins to serve only lunch to the local working class.

It is sometime during the Christmas holidays that Susan is surprised by Jacob's coming home early one night and being interested in sex. The surprise, the anger, and the resentment that she feels make her want to refuse. But the starvation that she feels causes her to comply.

In the end, an argument ensues, and Jacob says to her, "It's only because my woman is unavailable tonight why I've come here anyway."

Susan doesn't allow the incident to crush her spirit. "Although she can't fall asleep long after he has rolled over and is fast asleep, she calls on her friend, Jesus. And she feels His caresses across her shoulders, which put her to sleep."

> *"Although she can't fall asleep long after he has rolled over and is fast asleep, she calls on her friend, Jesus. And she feels His caresses across her shoulders, which put her to sleep."*

When she awakes in the morning she has no recollection of the night's incident, but as it gradually comes back to her, she just dismisses it as a bad dream and continues with her busy schedule.

Being so preoccupied with work and children and the burdens of her life, Susan fails to realize that she has missed a period. When one day at work she sits down in the lounge for a break, she looks up at the calendar on the wall and thinks to herself that it is a long time since she has had a period. She goes home and checks her personal calendar and calculates that she is two months pregnant. She eventually goes to the doctor and has the pregnancy confirmed.

One morning when she is almost ready for work, Jacob is awake, and she decides to tell him. That evening he comes home, to her surprise again, with gallons of orange juice, cheese, and fruits. At this time, Susan doesn't feel so happy. In the nights when she lies in bed, she thinks, *Diapers. Bottles.* And tears just stream down her face.

Soon, though, the baby starts to move, and she has her usual feeling of well-being and starts to enjoy her pregnancy.

By spring 1985, the restaurant looks like a run-down corner food shop; customers complaining about the quality of the food; and Adassa and two helpers are sitting around most of the time. The bar and nightclub are thriving because the night bartender is still on the job, in spite of Adassa's presence. The drugstore is closed. Its customers complain that it was a good thing, and they miss it. It prevented them from having to go into the capital for all their pharmaceutical needs.

At this time, Jacob is busy with his next phase of development—the marina. He has applied for and gained water rights for all the water bordering his property, so now he is about to develop into the sea.

He makes many trips overseas and frequently entertains business associates. When he returns, he is loaded with toys and games and books for the children and perfumes for Susan. He usually asks Susan if she missed him. Although she tries to explain that he doesn't have to go away for her to miss him, that she misses him even when he is supposedly at home, he doesn't seem to get it because he asks again without trying to do anything to improve the situation.

As he entertains at home, he invites her out to dinner often, and they dine in the best restaurants and hotels. All the previous conditions still exist, but she is living above them. She puts aside all her negative feelings and enjoys the social life, always hoping and praying that Jacob will come to his senses soon. When business associates bring their families, they stay for the weekend, and Jacob takes his family with his guests for poolside lunch at hotel restaurants. The children play together, and they all go in the pool. At such times, Jacob attends fully to the children, and Susan just relaxes.

One Sunday afternoon in the summer, Susan, now well advanced in her pregnancy, feels like going out with the children for some entertainment. At the same time, Jacob's foreman comes looking for Jacob, who is not at home. He stays to chat, as he usually does on such occasions, and to see if Jacob will arrive. Susan is well in the mood for entertainment, and she feels like she wants to go to the business and demonstrate to Adassa and exercise her position in the whole mix of things. She invites Jacob's foreman to accompany her. She dresses in a fine lounge suit and dresses the children nicely, and they all go to the business.

As the four of them enter the restaurant, Adassa is there all by herself, looking tired and worn and unkempt. The adults greet her, and she moves toward the children, greeting them and telling them, "I am your mammy."

The children ignore her because they do not know her.

Susan proceeds to the refrigerator in the bar to get some drinks. In no time, Adassa comes at her with a piece of lumber in her hand raised high and saying, "I can just put you out of here with this piece of stick I have in my hand."

Susan just stands boldly in front of her and tells her, "T-r-y it! T-r-y it!"

Adassa retreats, saying, "I glad he pop her up again. I hope after this one, he will pop her up with another one."

Susan has guessed right that she would need a witness. They all just sit in the lounge area and have their drinks. Feeling satisfied that her message is received and pleased at the way Adassa chooses to portray herself to the children, Susan leaves, smiling.

It is September, and both Angeline and Nicholas are in kindergarten. Angeline has already spent one year, and Nicholas has just started. They come home at midday. Nicholas is actually too young, but for the whole year, he cried in the mornings to go with Angeline. He would take her lunch kit and strut around the house with it and make a fuss when it came time to give it up. With the new baby coming, Susan wanted to make sure he didn't regress, so she asked the principal if he could attend. The school concluded that he was ready, so the principal accepted him in school.

On September 28, a third child is born to Jacob and Susan. He is a boy, and they name him Stephen.

Susan enjoys her three months maternity leave, resting and doing activities with the children. Some days during the week, after the children's afternoon nap, they all and Carol go to the beach. Susan floats on her back in the sea and thanks God for a good life.

When she sees that her third child is a boy, Susan is ecstatic. Her deepest heart's desire has been to have three children, two boys and one girl. She has never put this desire into conscious thought or words. She is so excited she can hardly believe her blessing. She thinks how God has seen into the depths of her heart and granted her desire without her even asking. She is truly grateful. She wanted two boys and a girl because she has seen from young the situation in families—how fathers are mostly absent or at least have very little positive influence in the home. She reasoned that the girl would have her as a feminine role model. If the father were absent, whether physically or otherwise, the boys would have each other to put their heads together and work out the male thing. She thinks that God agrees with her logic, and although she was ready to settle for the first two children, He has given her her real desire. She marvels at how He Himself has brought about the third one.

Life with Jacob has not improved in any way. Their relationship with each other has not grown. Jacob does not seem to be open to any kind of change in himself, and he chooses to invest himself in somebody else. As for his financial contribution, Susan feels he is just meeting some obligation he feels he has.

So one day, at the end of her maternity leave, she says to him, "Well, I have all my children now. You can go now and do with yourself just what you want."

"Oh! So you were only using me!" he exclaims pitifully.

Susan is so surprised. She never thought that he had feelings. After all, he has never treated her as if she is a person and with feelings. She almost feels sorry for him, but she reminds herself that he has never shown any sympathy for the way she must feel.

At the same time, she is thinking that something needs to change. She wishes that there were someone who could have a talk with Jacob. She wants now to seek outside help for her situation, and she considers that the person must be someone whom Jacob respects. She thinks of this outstanding lawyer in the community named Robert Aldrin, whom everyone thinks highly of. He is always asked to address gatherings, even ladies clubs and church groups. He even gave an address at the opening ceremony of Jacob's nightclub, bar and restaurant in the capital. He is always commenting on legal and political issues and always in the news, especially on radio.

She gets an appointment to see him. She sits in his office and relates her entire story to him, and he tells her he will talk with Jacob and then see her again. He prepares a letter for Jacob, which she agrees to deliver, and she does.

As she waits anxiously to hear from Robert Aldrin, one night Jacob comes home early and laughs at her for having talked to a lawyer. He even says, "And Mr. Aldrin has a letter for you, but as I am not your mailman, I didn't take it."

Susan is crushed. She waits, but she never hears from Robert Aldrin.

Her goal continues to be to raise stable, responsible, and emotionally healthy children, even in spite of the shortcomings of her family. She teaches them at home; they learned numbers, letters, colors, and their names before they entered kindergarten. She teaches them concrete mathematical concepts, which she fears may be lacking in the classroom, and she teaches them phonetics and reading at home to supplement whatever they learn in school. She lets them explore outdoors and, in conversation, teaches them reasoning and logical thinking. In their relationship with each other, she teaches them love, compassion, and responsibility for their actions. And this is how life continues on a daily basis in the Wells household, with Susan in her usual lifestyle and Jacob usually absent.

Christmas comes and is celebrated in their traditional way at home. Stephen is one year old and walking. Angeline is six and in primary school. She has started to attend all day. Nicholas is four and reading. In preparation for the holidays, Jacob has decided to take the family to Puerto Rico for shopping and to have the children take pictures with Santa. They spend four nights in a fine hotel and enjoy its amenities; Jacob takes the children into the swimming pool while Susan spends time by herself in the gym and in the spa.

Grandmother's health is deteriorating, and she doesn't leave her bed anymore. So Susan takes the children to visit her on Boxing Day.

Jacob's younger siblings are in high school. His brother gets into trouble occasionally, and when Adassa is called to the school, Jacob has to walk at her side as the father figure. He has to support her and her younger children while she works shoulder to shoulder with him in his business, in Susan's opinion, like they are spouses.

Chapter 5

WHAT WILL BECOME OF THE CHILDREN?

It is May 1987. Jacob is ready to open the second phase of his development, the marina. Apart from the berths out in the sea equipped with water and electricity for boats to dock at, there are on-land showers and toilets and spaces for shops and offices to serve the boaters. One weekend, Jacob tells Susan that, on Wednesday of the following week, he is going to clean the building with the offices in preparation for them to be occupied.

Wednesday night arrives, and Susan has the three children ready for bed when she thinks of Jacob cleaning the building all by himself. With the children, she is unable to do much to help, but she decides to load them into her car and drive into the capital to lend support. When she arrives at the site, she sees s woman named Tina Chambers from her neighborhood inside cleaning the windows. She has had reasons to believe that Tina Chambers was one of Jacob's women. She doesn't want to jump to conclusions, so she enters the building with the children and goes to where Jacob is.

"How much are you paying this woman?" she asks.

He doesn't look at the family or acknowledge their presence for a good three minutes. She looks directly at him for the entire three

39

minutes and then just leaves and goes home to puts her children to bed.

The next morning on her way to work, she packs some dirty clothes for Jacob in a laundry bag and leaves them at Tina Chambers' apartment door with a note saying, "Here. Now that you have finished the cleaning, it's time to do the laundry."

Since that Wednesday night, Susan frequently thinks, at bedtime, of Adassa in the capital, wearing herself out in the business while she, Susan, is in the comfort of her clean home with her little children in bed. She thinks how it should have been her stressing to help her husband to support her home, but instead she has fools working for her. She just smiles and goes to sleep. Occasionally, whenever she feels like it, she just walks into the business, with or without the children, in the daytime or at night when she gets Carol to babysit. The staff knows her and gives her due recognition, and Adassa can only look on in dismay.

Also in May, Susan attends a Sunday afternoon tea party with the children. As the four of them sit at a table, she looks around and sees adults at their table talking to each other. She begins to feel awkward sitting with three little children. She sees a group of dancers providing entertainment. She decides that she will enquire about the group. When Stephen is two years old, she will join the group. She reasons that dancing in the group will have multiple benefits. It will be her regular exercise, will provide entertainment, and will also provide adult companionship.

The following month, Carol, the helper, gets married. Carol asks Susan to use her car and be the chauffer to transport her to the church and her and her husband from the church to the reception. Carol gets her cousin to transport and tend the children and to work in her place while she goes on her honeymoon.

When school closes for summer at the end of June, Nicholas's teacher tells Susan that Nicholas has been accepted for primary school in September. She says the principal of Angeline's primary school came to test potential six-year-old pupils for transfer, so she didn't consider Nicholas. But Nicholas's teacher told the principal that Nicholas can read and that he is a mature and independent worker; his time would be wasted there with her for another school year. So the principal tested Nicholas and was very impressed and accepted him. Susan is a little concerned about Nicholas moving at such a fast pace, but she finds him mature herself, and she is ready to do whatever is necessary to support him.

This year, Susan takes her vacation in the summer. She takes the month of July. Nicholas's teacher is having summer school the second and third weeks of July, and Susan registers Angeline and Nicholas. After a week of rest for herself and the school-age children, Susan takes Angeline and Nicholas to summer school in the mornings and returns home. She takes Stephen with her to pick them up at midday, and instead of returning home immediately, the four of them have lunch at their favorite hotel restaurant where there is a children's pool. After lunch, they walk in the garden, where the children enjoy the plants and flowers and even find insects. Then the children have fun together in the kiddie pool. And that is how they spend the next two weeks.

Susan erects a notice board in the living room and displays the children's artwork form summer school.

She has begun to enjoy and appreciate Jacob's absence from the home. Whenever he is at home, he undermines her training of the children. The children try to engage in unacceptable behavior, and she, Susan, has to engage in more disciplining, which is more work for her. During the summertime, the children are allowed to watch much television, and they can observe a later bedtime. When their father is around, though, they tend to waste food, throw their clothes and toys around on the floor, and make a fuss about not going to bed and are generally uncooperative. They just want to be disorderly and with him, now that he shows a little more interest in them as they get older.

In fact, Jacob takes Angeline and Nicholas with him regularly for grocery shopping, and sometimes Susan goes also with Stephen. The children are allowed to pick out whatever they wish, and the older ones pick out the cereals they see advertised on television with toys in the boxes. They also pick out lots of candies, which Susan has to supervise and control the eating of when they get home. As for the cereal, after they have taken the toys from the boxes, they have no interest in it. So Susan's work with the children is tedious because of Jacob's laxness.

As the months have rolled by, with Jacob very busy with the second phase of his development, the first phase has suffered neglect and deteriorated. Jacob finds a suitable tenant and leases out the restaurant, bar, and nightclub. Adassa becomes the cleaner for the new offices and showers and toilets. It amazes Susan that she chooses to be a cleaner in Susan's business rather than to be owner and manager of her own business. But presumably, when a person has one goal in life, he or she will do whatever it takes in an attempt to accomplish that goal. And Adassa's goal is to displace Susan.

The New Year arrives, and Stephen is almost two and a half years old. Angeline and Nicholas are doing very well in primary school—earning between 95 and 100 percent on tests. Angeline is at the top of her class and on the honor roll.

Susan is an active member of the parent-teacher association, and she is appalled at the problems in the school with difficult pupils. She also gets information from Nicholas and Angeline about the kinds of things that happen in their classrooms. One day Nicholas reports that a problematic pupil in his class kicked the teacher. Angeline talks about the sexual conversations that take place among her classmates. Susan also gets information from the local news about outrageous happenings in the high school, and she sees the behavior and hears the speech of the high school students on the streets.

She continues to read the Bible and relevant books and articles to obtain facts and opinions with which to compare and contrast her own ideas. She continues to spend her wakeful predawn hours writing down her thoughts since she has no other outlet for them.

Susan also discovers that the dancers she saw at the tea party belong to a group called the Cultural and Rhythm Dancers. She learns the details of their meetings and activities and joins the group. Now she goes dancing every Monday evening at seven to ten o'clock, while Carol, although she is married, agrees to babysit.

It takes some two months before Jacob discovers that she is going out on Monday nights, and he starts coming home early enough to see when she arrives home. Susan finds it amusing that suddenly he finds the time to come home. But after Carol leaves, he curses her and accuses her of being out with a man. He feels his presence will frighten her and make her stop. When she ignores him and continues her dancing, he starts calling her a whore and cursing her, saying that she is on the streets taking a man, while he is busy working hard for her and the children.

Susan finds it all amusing. She enjoys her dancing, which is one activity that solves three of her problems, namely, providing exercise, entertainment and adult companionship. Sometimes Jacob dismisses Carol before Susan gets home, and when Susan arrives, he is there with the children asleep. Susan is enjoying herself so much on Monday nights. The children are now accustomed to her leaving them the one night per week, and they are fast asleep when she gets home. So she stops rushing home after dancing. She sometimes sits around with the other members of the group laughing and talking until midnight. When she does not want to talk, she stops at a favorite hotel bar for her favorite drinks of daiquiri or ginger ale and brandy or milk and brandy.

Jacob continues to spy on what time she arrives home and to curse her and call her a whore. Sometimes he curses her on the weekend in the presence of the children. She mostly ignores him because she wonders with which mouth and tongue he calls her a whore.

When sometimes she feels troublesome, she asks him, "Am I a mirror that, when you look at me, you see yourself and think you are talking to yourself?"

Or she will ask, "Are you sure you are not talking to your mother?"

But the name-calling begins to hurt her deeply. One weekend when he calls her a whore, she responds, "And a very proud one!"

Well, he raises his hand and gives her a slap across the face and hits her in the head a few times with his fists. She goes straight to the police station, which is nearby, and reports the incident. Then she returns home and calms and comforts the children, by which time he leaves.

About the middle of the same year, Susan notices that she has lots of pages of notes, all of which she has recorded in her wakeful predawn hours. She reviews them one day. Her thoughts become organized. One early morning while she is awake, she writes a long composition. She reviews it the following day and titles it "Dear Fathers." At the first opportunity, she gives a copy of it to Jacob to read.

A whole week passes, and he says absolutely nothing to her. But Susan is intent on being heard, so she prepares the composition into a commentary and takes it to the editor of her favorite newspaper.

Meanwhile, Jacob has made a habit of coming home when he feels like it on a Monday night, dismissing the babysitter when he feels like it, and hitting Susan in her head and calling her names in the night or on the weekend. When he curses her, she ignores him. But every time he hits her, she goes to the police station and makes a formal report. Then she has to extract the children from wherever they are hiding and try to mend their broken spirits.

They go out to lunch and the swimming pool on Saturdays or Sundays after church. She constantly encourages them not to worry but just to learn their lessons in school, so that, when they are big, they can get a good job and be able to take care of themselves. Then they can make a happy family of their own, and then they will forget all of this unhappiness.

A few times after Susan's police report, a pair of policemen has come to try to speak with Jacob. But he has refused each time to converse with them, chasing them from his home and telling them they are intruding and must cease from interfering in his private family life.

On one occasion, he curses Susan in the presence of the policemen and the children and kicks her. The children hide themselves under the dining table. The policemen try to reason with him and leave after they are unsuccessful. After that occasion, Jacob adds a new curse to the barrage of insults he slings at her, saying that she is having an affair with the policemen.

The year continues in that erratic way and ends with the family going to Puerto Rico for Christmas shopping and the children receiving all the toys and games they desire and nice clothes as well. They all enjoy themselves in their favorite hotel, and all this is at absolutely no cost to Susan.

When they return home, plans for the Christmas celebrations are moderate because there are two funerals to think about. Jacob's maternal grandmother, whom the children know, and Susan's paternal grandmother, whom the children do not know, both died recently and will be buried in the same month—the month of December. Jacob is somewhat saddened by his grandmother's death, as she raised him while his mother was being the breadwinner for his family. Susan and the children attend the funeral with him before Christmas.

Susan is not saddened by her grandmother's death; although she knew her grandmother and had seen her several times, she was never close to her. She had learned from her mother of the many things that her grandmother had done to undermine her parents' marriage and to sow disharmony in her home as a child. Her grandmother had broken her home from its very beginning, much the way Jacob's mother had done to her grandchildren. Some of the things Susan's grandmother had done were exactly like those Jacob's mother had done. So Susan has no plans to go so far away to attend the funeral.

However, the weekend before the funeral, Susan calls her parents' home. Her father is crying because his mother is dead. So the day before the funeral, she takes the train by herself and goes back home to attend the funeral. At church, she sits with her mother in the back. Now she can identify with her mother's feelings, which she expressed over the years.

While the mourners go to the graveside, she and her mother go to a local restaurant for drinks at the bar. Susan tells her mother that she will be working to overcome her emotional wounds and that she hopes they don't last a lifetime as in her mother's case. She knows that, if she and Jacob were able to mend their marriage and family life, she would forget all that has gone before. But it would take the two of them to accomplish it.

She returns home and is very reflective. She realizes that Jacob has his own emotional problems, which makes him unable to give of himself. He is only practicing what he has learned over the years. However, she doesn't excuse him for not seeking to improve himself; he knows right from wrong, and he is the one who chooses to do wrong. She pledges to herself there and then to cease to contribute anything to the dysfunction in her home and to pray and fast for her family and all the individuals in it and for her marriage. She refuses to allow her children to continue in a violent environment, and she pledges to be a peacemaker and an example to Jacob. Thus, a very erratic year ends in hope.

Chapter 6

SOME NEWSPAPER COMMENTARIES

The editor of Susan's favorite newspaper is female, and Susan is happy about that. She thinks a female will be more receptive to what she has written and more likely to print it. The editor reads the article and loves it. She publishes it in the following week's newspaper. The commentary reads:

Dear Fathers
By Susan Wells

I think most honest people, if not all, would agree with the statement that fathers are what is wrong with families today. If this is so, then men are what is wrong with the community at large. Why aren't men addressed on this topic more? Is it because everyone is afraid to touch the subject? Is it because men are more frequently the speakers? And is it because the subject is not properly addressed that the situation remains as it is? Everybody knows that families, on the whole, are not what they are supposed to be. Is this nation concerned about the matter or not? Need I repeat the value of families to a nation?

Why can't men be better fathers? Because they are not better husbands either. I know some cases where men in families want to be good fathers to their children without being good husbands. But I say that this is not possible. If the father does not love and respect the mother of his children, how are the children going to be happy? And how is he going to teach them about a healthy male-female relationship, one of the greatest sources of happiness in life? The greatest love a man can show to his children is to love their mother. I say that the two roles are inseparable, and they mark a good and successful man.

Many men seem to think that success means to be successful in business, political, and career adventures at the expense of their families. But I would like to see the day when men's organizations and the community at large communicate, even in some subtle way, to men that, to be truly successful means to be successful in both of their two basic roles—as career personnel and as head of their homes. It has long been recognized that the working woman has two careers, but it seems to me that men are born with two careers, notwithstanding that most can only perceive one.

Many men fail at home. (And do you realize that, somehow, it is subtly communicated that it is the women who fail?) But the man is the head of the home, and whether it is failure or success, the responsibility is his. So many men fail because they try to lead their families long-distantly, sometimes from the house or the bed of some woman on the street. I would say that this is a very intricate matter, which could only be unraveled with proper education of wives and husbands alike. Maybe it would even also require education of the women on the streets, whose "deep pits" the husbands fall into. (Proverbs 22:14 reads, "The mouth of a strange woman is a deep pit: he that is abhorred of the Lord shall fall therein.")

So you see, men, it is not because something is wrong with your wives. Here I would like to quote Dr. James Dobson from his book *What Wives Wish Their Husbands Knew about Women*: "If I had the power to communicate only one message to every family in America, I would specify the importance of romantic love to every aspect of feminine existence. It provides the foundation for a woman's self-esteem, her joy in living, and her sexual responsiveness. Therefore the vast number of men who are involved in bored, tired marriages—and who find themselves locked out of the bedroom—should know where the trouble possibly lies. Real love can melt an iceberg." Doesn't this quotation throw the ball in the men's court, where it belongs? For America we can substitute any nation.

This important puzzle unraveled to men can also provide the foundation for better families, thus better citizens and a better nation. Do we care or don't we? Then I would like to recommend that husbands who are truly interested in becoming good fathers should read this book. And yes, of course, you can show it to your wives. But more importantly, give it to your sons. Teach them to be the leaders where you have failed. I am, therefore, advocating that the way to become a good father is through being a good husband.

At this point, I must commend the many women-led groups that are making a special effort to give the needed education to women and men alike and the several other voices that call men to be educated in the ways of family living. But the sad point is that I don't think that the voices can reach the men who most need the education, because these particular men have a problem that is called "macho image." And it is most unlikely that these men will be seen in places where such information is given. It is for this reason that I would like to call the attention of the more macho organizations, like the different men's clubs, to bring this information to your members. And at the same time I would like to ask why is it that these organizations are so often addressed on topics of political, economic, and entrepreneurial interests and never on family matters? Why is it that women are so often addressed on these matters through lectures, plays, and skits at functions and that a woman's organization would always address the topic of family and the role of women and children but rarely, if ever, a male organization will address the topic of family life and the role of men as leaders in the home? Is it because even men of substantially high statue in the community do not recognize this role? Or is it just that they do not understand its implications?

There is a solution for heads of families (that is, husbands and fathers) who are spending valuable family time hiding and lurking in dark places and in the 'deep pits' I have mentioned. Put their role on stage in plays and skits and let them see themselves. Let the community show displeasure and dissatisfaction. Are we displeased or dissatisfied?

On the other hand, at the same time show in plays and skits the role we expect them to play. Here I would like to exclude the few men who uphold high moral standards and who are leading their homes like real masculine stalwarts. These I would say are real men. I close here by saying, men, even if you don't love your wife, and you should—it is a law of God (Ephesians 5:25, "Husbands love your wives")—be kind to your children and stop embarrassing them. Women on the streets, help the men!

Women of statute in the community respond favorably to the commentary in the newspaper, and Susan learns that they are silenced by their husbands. Susan realizes that, if all men were cheaters but they had no women to cheat with, men could not cheat. But instead, a woman will pursue her friend's male companion or even her own sister's husband. Even mothers-in-law and sisters-in-law can make life very difficult for a wife. Some women just don't like to see another woman enjoy life. This is especially true of women who have been rejected by a man.

On the other hand, men respect each other's boundaries. Men support each other in ways women do not. There are men who would rather say right is wrong or wrong is right than say that their buddy did wrong. Susan decides to address the women also in the following newspaper commentary:

Dear Mothers
By Susan Wells

If the woman hastily agrees that fathers have relinquished their leadership role in families, and if women hastily accept the credit for holding down the fort in such periods of crisis, then the woman must now hastily accept the responsibility for failure in the home.

Nonetheless, I say this with great sympathy and understanding. After all, if a certain engine is built to run on oil and, in the absence of oil, we get it to perform with water, then we do feel some gratitude and pride for getting the engine to perform at all. The family was designed by its engineer (God) to be led by a man. The woman substitute for leadership has done much to cause boys to be unprepared to lead when they establish their own families as men. Already we see the pattern of a vicious cycle. New families will, in turn, be led by women, and new males will be produced and raised again unprepared for leadership.

In order to break this vicious cycle, the woman will have to display a certain bravery and skill, which she must find deep within.

In the midst of great frustrations—sexual, financial, and emotional and even physical abuse—with the greatest love that exists next only to godly love, a mother's love, the woman must live above her personal pains and sufferings and look beyond, to a better future for her children. We have already proved in our communities that a better future is not promised in the schooling of our children and in the securing of future financial comfort for them. It is my opinion that a brighter future is promised in happier homes and in a more stable and loving and original family structure. Why are louder voices (leading men's voices) not calling men to create better families?

In the absence of male leadership, there is much that the woman can do. And I ask mothers: You have known the pain and sufferings of feminine needs unmet. Why have you not taught your sons to be good husbands? Many a mother entertains hopes of keeping her son to herself to fill some of the vacuum left by the boy's father. Many a mother hates the thought of a daughter-in-law who will have the joys of life from her son that she missed from his father. And this is only one of the ways in which women break each other. But I say that the mothers who take these positions are far crueler and more selfish than the men who have abandoned their seats at the head of families and whose greatest crime may be ignorance.

On the other hand, many mothers do not fully understand the sufferings they bear. They hurt tremendously and cannot identify the source of their pain, nonetheless express it. Tim and Beverly LaHaye, in their book *The Act of Marriage*, identify five different kinds of love that a woman needs. These are companionship love, compassionate love, romantic love, affectionate love, and passionate love. And the men who bypass all these on their way to their own physical sexual relief, the LaHayes refer to as "sexual illiterates." Sir, this is what your wife has been trying to tell you all these years while you have been shouting, "Nag! Nag! Nag!"

This is not for you to feel too good now, ladies. You have not heard from your husbands what their needs of love are either. I know they have not taken the time out to explain them to you, and I know you have been waiting a long time for your husbands, as the head of the home to start the education of the family. So now we all understand what the counselors have been saying when they have been shouting, "Communicate! Communicate! Communicate!"

What I would really like to communicate is that many bookstores carry the books I have mentioned and many other books to suit the specific needs of individual families. I would also like to communicate to mothers that it now lies in their hands to change the future for their children, even if it is too late for a better life for themselves.

When I say mothers, I am inevitably addressing two categories of women. There is the wife at home with her children, and there is the woman on the streets hounding the husbands. The possession of the children renders the wife disadvantaged, while the woman on the streets has left her children in the care of someone else in order to render herself a viable competitor. (Proverbs 28, read, "She also lieth in wait as for a prey, and increaseth the transgressors among men.") Both these women have the same feminine needs and frustrations, and both are now with a set of fatherless children as the husband hangs between them like a piece of bread. (In Proverbs 6:26, "For by means of a whorish woman a man is brought to a piece of bread.")

I must, however, separate these mothers because they both exist to the disadvantage of each other. And this is another proof that a woman's greatest enemy is another woman. I know men who still like to shout, "I am the head," and, "I am the boss." But can a piece of bread lead in the home?

To the wives, I would like to say gather strength and courage, because the women on the streets have been around for a long time, and we can believe that they are here to stay. (Proverbs 5:3–4, says, "For the lips of a strange woman drops as a honeycomb, and her mouth is smoother than oil: but her end is bitter as worm-wood.) These women on the streets also serve a vital function. They are the means by which some husbands spite their wives for their own inability to lead their home and for their lack of knowledge of the implications of such leadership. So, ladies, if you would like the women on the streets to disappear, you will have to train your sons to be leaders in their own homes and not followers in yours. It is because, in the absence of fathers, mothers have taught their sons to follow them that husbands follow the women on the streets, who are always there to lead them on. (In Proverbs 22:3, "A prudent man foreseeth the evil, and hideth himself: but the simple pass on, and are punished.")

The fact that the women of communities are they who have seen that a problem exists in families today and that the women have taken the lead to study the situation and educate themselves and that the women are now calling the men to educate themselves also is enough proof that women are in the lead. Ladies leading in the home, please be ready to make room when the men do appear. Here there is much that can be said.

There are, for example, a variety of arrangements that can be identified. Some women enter the situation with the intention of simply sharing another woman's husband, having him to meet some of their feminine needs and to be a father figure to some child they may have without a father in the child's life. They do not wish to break up the family. They are very discrete and humble. Other women enter the situation with the intention of gaining the husband for themselves. They call the man's home and try to identify themselves and seek opportunity to create discord in the home. Some husbands are very discrete and don't tolerate a woman who tries to disturb his home. And, as I said, a variety of arrangements exist.

But I close with consolation to the hearts of women. It is generally another woman who is at the root of all your troubles. Women suffer because they are each other's enemies, unlike men, who support each other. Mothers at home, remember that many a woman on the streets is seeking a father for her fatherless children. Women on the streets, remember you are creating a new set of fatherless children. Here the men can feel proud that the women look up to them as possessing the answers to their problems. But, mothers, only through the pages of the Holy Bible will you find the answers that you have been seeking in the weak flesh of weak men.

Susan has observed that, in dysfunctional families, the children are the ones who suffer the most. The greatest pain they suffer is emotional, and this pain can continue long after any other pain has ceased. Their parents suffer emotional pain also. This pain is experienced very deep in one's being and is very often lifelong. The children hurt for themselves, but they also hurt for their parents' unhappiness. Sometimes both parents are hurting when there is quarrelling and fighting in the home. Sometimes only one parent is hurting when one of the parents is being unfaithful and enjoying it.

Susan thinks that family is a community institution and so is marriage; she believes the community could do a lot more to build the family as the basic unit of the nation. The community needs to be proactive rather than reactive and start to prepare children from early in school for a happy family life of their own.

If the nation is, as it calls itself, a Christian nation, it should teach its children to find true and basic information in the Bible about how the family is supposed to work and not in books that men have made to impart their own faulty ideas. She thinks that even the government and lawmakers should seek their guidance and solutions for the nation's social problems from the Word, rather than from so-called developed nations whose devastating outcomes are obvious.

Since the father in the situations discussed are not nurturing the family and the mothers, in the absence of the fathers, are not covering the children, Susan decides to address the children in her next newspaper commentary. She writes:

Dear Children
By Susan Wells

My first question to you is why do so many young people follow blindly and make the same mistakes that so many of your parents have made? If you look closely, you will see that nations follow nations and follow the same pitfalls. But those who dream of a better life will have to do things differently than did most of the people who went before them. Most people, even from very young, have dreams of being a member of a happy family. Regardless of career and other dreams, most people expect to be members of happy and prosperous families sometime in their future; and the more successful one becomes in the other areas of life, the greater is the wish for family life to share the joys and pleasures. This being so, most people put tremendous effort into preparing to meet the demands of career and other adventures. But how many put equal effort into preparing for the role he or she will play in his or her own family?

When people were first created, their only purpose on earth was to love God and one another. Man and woman were placed on earth, and their supreme work was to share their love and enjoy the fruits of this love, which are children. (In Genesis 1:28, "Be fruitful and multiply and replenish the earth.")

This seems to suggest, therefore, that man's basic purpose on earth was to have a family. But because of sin, all work has been made more difficult, even the work of making a family. (Genesis 3:19, "In the sweat of thy face shall thou eat bread.") All this suggests that every human being was created to be a member of a happy family. Why then don't more people prepare themselves for a happy family life?

The first thing a young person can do is to look closely at the family in which he or she lives; see the things that are right and wrong, good and bad; and try to understand the reasons and causes. Most young people find faults with their parents; why then do you move on to be the same kind of parents? Many girls and boys, for example, live with mothers; they do not know or cannot find their fathers. Many girls and boys face the pain, embarrassment, and humiliation of meeting strangers in school who they must call brothers and sisters. Many other situations arise because of the absence and/or philandering of fathers that bring to children daily and often relentless frustration. Yet your only response is to do the same thing to your own children. Why is this so? It is a vicious cycle that only the young ones now have the power to break. Would anyone like to do it for your children?

Those who wish to make a better life for their children will first have to understand the nature of human beings, so as to understand themselves and the people around them. This is the only way they can enable themselves to grow into strong, healthy, wise individuals.

Would you like to be wise? The book of Proverbs in the Bible tells you how to be wise. Now, one part of wisdom is to understand the four basic areas of human nature. Every person has four areas of his or her being that have been designed to grow. These four areas, however, need four different kinds of food and four different kinds of exercise to cause proper growth and development. And the starvation of any of the four areas will cause that particular area to be deformed. Some young people who are experiencing unhappiness, frustrations, and poor general feelings are suffering from the effects of deformity of one or more of the four areas of your being.

It is most unlikely that you are unknowingly suffering from deformity of your physical being (your body). You can easily recognize this area and its needs. You feel hungry. You eat. Since most normal, healthy people have a constant desire to eat food and are willing to satisfy that desire (some are unable), the body continues to grow. Notice, however, how different bodies look according to the kinds of food the individuals eat and the amount of exercise they get?

This means, then, that the deformity more likely exists in one or more of the other three areas, which are your intellect (your mind), your emotion (your feelings), and your spirit (your soul). These three areas are similar to the body in that their endurance reflects the quality and quantity of food and exercise they have received. When a person is not fully developed in all four areas of his or her being, the individual is unstable and unbalanced. He or she is like a four-legged table with one or two or three legs short.

After the physical, the next area you will recognize is the intellect. Your parents send you to school to feed and exercise your mind in order to develop it. Some of you do a very good job.

The third area you should recognize, and you don't, is the spiritual; many parents send you to church also. They do so to feed and exercise your soul and cause it to grow healthily. Oh! Now you know why you go to school and church.

The fourth area, which should be more difficult to recognize and which most of you readily recognize, is the emotional. Sadly, though, you think it is purely sexual. Many of your parents have hardly given you any food or exercise for your emotions. Some of them have given you poisonous food and strenuous exercise, and your emotions are in need of medicine and care.

Most of your parents, however, have given you all of the best food and exercise that they have had available, which in many cases have been insufficient. But because you recognize your emotions and they feel hungry, you search for your own food. As I have said, you recognize your emotions as purely sexual. Therefore, you feel satisfied by the sexual exposure that you find on television and in certain books, magazines, movies, and company. This causes you to have sexual relations early and sometimes have a child very early in life; this is where many family troubles begin.

But emotions are a lot more than sex. They involve a variety of complex feelings and responses that you should learn about if you wish to be a happier and stronger person. And a strong emotional being, along with a strong spiritual nature make up the depth of one's being. These are the major aspects of self that will help an individual build a satisfying family life.

Susan then thinks of the problems that children bring into the schools, and she has a very puzzling question in her head. She decides to ask it in her fourth newspaper commentary. This is what she writes:

What's Going on at Home?
By Susan Wells

I have more questions, I'm sorry to say. My next question is what's going on at home? As I learn of the many problems of some of the children in the classroom and see the behavior of the majority of them on the streets, I cannot help wondering why these children and young people must be seeking help and attention outside of their homes. What role are some of the homes playing in the lives of their children?

It becomes evident that some of the homes are destroying, rather than building, their own children. The majority of children leave their homes in a state of grave instability. Many of them are rough, crude, angry, hostile, and hateful, without any tenderness, care, consideration, or love, not to mention deeper thinking. Yet they wear pretty shoes, fancy hairstyles, and often makeup on their faces and jewelry on their bodies. They definitely have money in their pockets. Such children certainly do not show a balanced development of the four areas of their personality—spiritual, emotional, intellectual, and physical. Such children show that their parents have either failed to recognize their responsibility to promote and guide their children's total and proper development or that they are just too selfish to care.

We have seen that the nation has taken a serious view of its role in the intellectual development of its children, and schools are provided strategically at all levels. The government takes on the responsibility of providing transportation for schoolchildren from home to school. And the government, as well as private enterprises, provides education at every level of the educational system. As a result of this, parents, I can safely say that the nation has taken up its responsibility in your child's intellectual development.

The doors of the churches are open wide every Saturday and Sunday and many weekdays also, and most churches provide free transportation for their members. So I can safely say that the churches are available to help parents in the spiritual development of your children.

As for physical development, children can help themselves from an early age and, sadly enough, many have to, however poorly.

At this point, we still have left the emotional development. Can parents name the institution that they think is responsible for their children's emotional development? Without this, the child is not complete. Would you believe that the full responsibility for this area of development lies at home? Is this why so many children are pretty on the outside and empty or ugly on the inside?

Not very much in life is perfect. Most if not all homes, I am sure, are imperfect. Let's face it, though. With a little sacrifice here and there, we can turn out better children than we are doing in most cases. I would not begin here to try to discuss the various problems that a home may be facing. But for every problem, there is some solution. I think that the major solution is present in the Book of Matthew. (Matthew 6: 33, reads, "Seek ye first the kingdom of God and his righteousness and all these things shall be added unto you.")

Dad, as head of the home, you are hereby called to the noble task of feeding your child's emotion. If Dad is on the streets and not even a fishing line can pull him in, Mom, can you take a little time? In between breadwinning, fortune building, socializing, fun gaining, grieving, and utter despairing, parents are called upon to seek to meet the needs of their children's emotions. The operative word is *seek*, as all those who seek will find.

This is a series of commentaries printed in Susan's favorite newspaper over a period of four months.

Chapter 7

A WIFE INFLUENCES THE LAWS OF HER COUNTRY

Susan continues to follow the news in the newspapers and on the radio. There are several commentaries on the chaotic situation that exists in many of the high schools and the danger some of the most unruly students pose to having a safe environment there. Many of the commentaries propose different solutions to the serious problems that exist, where fights have become more prevalent, among girls as well as boys, and students are bringing knives and other weapons to school.

The teachers and principals are pleading desperately for the government to take drastic measures to institute a system of expulsion for those students who are not making any progress academically and who are only being disruptive on a regular basis. The minister of education's only response is that nobody's child is going to be put out of school.

Susan recognizes that such a statement is only to secure votes in the next and subsequent elections. She decides to make her contribution in a letter to the editor. She writes:

Dear Madam,

Pursuant to the budget address of the week of April 18, I would like our nation and leaders of the nation to understand that, whereas in the past governments have taken the stand that nobody's child was going to be put out of school, it has since been recognized that this stand has been founded on misguided thinking and political maneuvering. Some governments, at least here in the Caribbean, have already started to change their position and to recognize the fact that discipline must be maintained in schools by means of a somewhat traditional system of punishment and reward. If we here in our country should take the first position, we would be way behind in human development, and we would have to experience many sad and serious events before we would be able to catch up with several other governments right here in the Caribbean.

The first position worked temporarily under irresponsible philosophies, such as "dispense with words like *bastard* and *illegitimate*" and institute "committed relationships" to substitute for marriage, a stand that fostered irresponsible parenting. But today, when parents are being called to resume their neglected responsibilities and there are still some parents who are seeking the very best for their children, not even parents are going to support this position. In our small country, parents hardly have a choice of place to send their children for secondary education. The more progressive thinking among them are going to be very annoyed at the thought of delinquent elements not only hampering the progress of their child's education, but also endangering the lives of the promising majority.

So the current thinking on the matter is to return to the old philosophy of not letting "one bad apple spoil the whole bunch." Whereas with apples we would simply discard the bad ones, with humans we must provide rehabilitation for our delinquents. I have read several suggestions in commentaries as to various proposals for handling delinquency in our public school system. Let me point out here that even the almighty and all-powerful God reserves hell and damnation in the next life for whomsoever may fail to utilize available opportunities to improve himself or herself in the present life. Thank you.

Very sincerely,
Susan Wells

Summer of the same year, the leader of the dance group plans a two-week Caribbean boat cruise for the dancers and their families. At the end of the cruise, the group will spend two nights in a hotel and one day at Disney World. Angeline is eight, Nicholas is six, and Stephen is three. School is out for summer vacation, and Susan takes some vacation time. Jacob works for himself. So he takes some time off to go on the cruise also. Susan has enough in savings to pay for the vacation, since she does not contribute to the running of the home. She spends most of her money on providing trips and entertainment for the children and herself during summer and Christmas school vacations.

There is lots of entertainment on the boat for the children to enjoy without their parents' supervision, and the older children take full advantage of it. They even enjoy much of the nightlife also.

Jacob is a man who sleeps all day and goes out at nights when he is not working. So this is what he does on the boat, where there is all-night entertainment and food. Susan attends shows and concerts during the day, at which events she "laughs her belly full" and "laughs her head off." At nights, she puts Stephen to bed, and she sleeps also. Jacob is not accustomed to spending time with Susan, and that does not change on the boat.

At the end of the boat cruise, the entire group checks into their hotel for two nights. The following day, they visit Disney World. Once in the hotel, Jacob begins to make suspicious telephone calls; those are certainly back home to his women. Of course this is very painful for Susan and almost spoils her vacation, except that she doesn't allow that to happen. She is very hurt and sad, however. She learns then that Jacob has neither respect nor compassion for her.

Two Monday nights following the vacation, the group does no dancing. Rather, everyone spends time reminiscing on the two weeks of fun they had. The boat stopped in Cozumel, Mexico; Ocho Rios, Jamaica; Grand Bahamas, Bahamas; and Grand Cayman, Cayman Islands.

The second Monday night they reminisce so much and Susan is having such a laugh that she forgets all about the time. When, eventually, she thinks of the time and looks, it is a quarter to one. She leaves the group and scurries home.

Carol's car is not outside when she arrives and Jacob's car is in the yard. She wonders what to expect. This is one of the few times in their marriage that she is arriving home, and her husband is at home, and she has never before arrived home this late. She is not prepared for what confronts her.

As she opens the front door with her key Jacob shouts, "Which man you were out with?"

He starts to hit her with a broomstick. He hits her on her arms and back and shoulders. She attempts to throw the telephone at him but thinks she will awaken the children.

Angeline wakes up anyway and comes out just in time to see her father leaving. Angeline is frightened to see the look of her mother. Susan's arms are swollen and bruised. She calms Angeline down and manages to get her to go back to sleep. Then she puts on the burglar alarm and leaves, walking to the police station, which is just across the street. She decides she is making her final report and tells the policemen that she has had enough of the reports. Now she wants the case to be heard in court.

It is half past three in the morning when Susan returns home. She puts a hot compress on her forehead and gets about three hours of sleep, waking before the children. She has to explain to them what has happened. She allows them to make breakfast for themselves before she drives them to school and takes Stephen along with her. She has called in sick for work so she goes straight to the doctor, who gives her two weeks sick leave.

When she returns home, Carol is surprised to see her and the condition of her arms. Carol puts ice on the bruises and makes her an early lunch, after which Susan has a good four hours of sleep. Carol offers to pick up Angeline and Nicholas so Susan can get some more rest and put more ice on the bruises.

In the evening, Susan allows the children to express how they feel. Stephen says he wishes he were bigger so he and Nicholas could hold down Daddy and beat him with a belt.

After two days of rest, Susan returns to the police station to enquire about the status of her case. She is told that the case has been referred to headquarters in the city, and the file has been sent.

After another two days, she goes to headquarters. She learns that the file was received and that the police officers are working on the case.

On four subsequent visits to headquarters over a period of two weeks, all that the policemen can tell her is that they are working on the case. So she goes to the attorney general's chambers and complains about the actions of the policemen, or rather, about their lack of action. The attorney general assigns Susan a lawyer from his chambers. The lawyer is female and shows herself to be quite knowledgeable of and sympathetic toward cases of domestic violence. She has one meeting with Susan and, in two weeks, informs Susan of a court date.

In the magistrate's court, the lawyer gives a lengthy presentation emphasizing the fact that victims of domestic violence are normally the only witnesses, as perpetrators of this crime do not normally perform their acts in the presence of other people. Jacob is represented by the aforementioned Robert Aldrin, whom you will hear more about later. Lawyer Aldrin tries to discredit Susan's integrity, emphasizing the point that she returned home after midnight, as if Jacob doesn't come home at three and four o'clock in the mornings. He tries to insinuate that Susan is an unfaithful wife, as if Jacob is not a blatantly unfaithful husband and as if either of those matters excuses violence.

At the end of two rather long presentations, the case is dismissed on the grounds that a wife is not allowed to testify against her husband.

Two weeks later, it is reported in the newspaper that the law has been changed to allow any victim of domestic violence to be able to testify in a court of law. The report outlines the recent case in the magistrate's court where a wife was willing to testify against her husband but was not allowed because of the previous law. Susan feels proud that she is able to induce positive change in her community, even at the lawmaking level.

This does not influence the relationship between her and Jacob any, except that he ceases to hit her or even to curse her. He continues in his same lowlife style, and she in her battle to raise emotionally healthy children and maintain a normal life for herself.

The children progress in their development. Angeline and Nicholas excel in primary school, and Stephen masters reading at an appropriate level. The year ends with Angeline nine, Nicholas seven, and Stephen four years old.

Christmas is celebrated as it was the previous year, in Puerto Rico and at home. On New Year's evening Jacob shows Susan a rough plan for their home and asks for her preferences and suggestions. The year 1990 passes uneventfully, except for the children's outstanding academic accomplishments and their trip to Canada in the summer with Susan.

Chapter 8

WILL THE HUSBAND BECOME A POLITICIAN?

It is January 1991. Stephen is in kindergarten, Nicholas is in class three, and Angeline is in class four. It is an election year. The campaigning has reached a high pitch, and the elections will take place in September. Jacob feels that it is his time to run for a seat in the House of Representatives. He has been campaigning since the previous year but has not discussed any of his activities with Susan. He has never asked her to attend any functions. The ruling party loves Jacob and is willing to welcome Jacob into its fold. The electorate of his community looks forward to making Jacob a local representative. The prime minister told Susan on one occasion, "Jacob will have whatever he wants." Jacob is well liked and respected by the common folk because he was raised very poor but did brilliantly in school and went overseas and got an advanced education. The electorate considers that Jacob has a lot to offer to the community and to the country.

In March, Angeline will participate in the finals of the Inter-Primary Schools Mathematics Quiz. The preliminaries took place in October of the precious year, and the semifinals were held in February. Of the twenty-five schools that entered the competition, Angeline's school is one of the five finalists. Angeline is on her school's team. March comes around, and Angeline's school takes second place in the championship. Each member of her team receives a medium-size trophy, and Angeline receives hers with pride. The whole family is proud and excited to hear the report on the local radio station. Angeline's name appears in the local newspaper, and Jacob receives congratulations from many members of the community. His pride is obvious.

Nicholas also makes his contribution to the family's pride. He is a valued member of his school's soccer team, scoring many goals in competitions. In April, Nicholas leads his school to first place in the Inter-Primary Schools Soccer Tournament. He plays midfield, and his knack of getting free makes him seems to always have the ball, with which he scores often. Each member of the champion team receives a large and elaborate trophy, and Nicholas is only too pleased to have a trophy to match with his sister. The family's pride is palpable. Again Jacob receives congratulations from the members of his community. But nothing in him tells him to respect his children and family with high moral conduct.

The Sunday that follows the game, Susan makes a formal dinner and sets the table with the children's favorite meal, stuffed Cornish hens, one for each person, and cupcakes and lots of ice cream. The children had to plead with their father to be present for dinner with the family.

Summer comes around, and it is the end of another school year. All three children have done very well at their lessons. Angeline and Nicholas are on the honor roll. Stephen has gotten an excellent end of year report. He receives a certificate declaring him the most loving pupil in his class. Everyone is so excited that Susan tells the children they can have a party and invite all their friends. They will call it a congratulations party. Lots of energy and enthusiasm go into the making and sending out of invitations and the planning of the menu.

All the preparations are done, and before July ends, the party takes place. All the invited guests arrive, and the party is a huge success. Everyone, even the adults—Susan; Carol; and Margret, the next-door neighbor—have a good time. All the children are very well behaved. They are very polite and display good etiquette around the food, to which everyone had free access.

September arrives, and the children are back in school. Nicholas's teacher decides to operate the class elections for class monitor as a national election. The candidates will campaign in class, and the pupils will vote on ballots. Nicholas is one of the candidates, and he and his father prepare speeches together. He wins his election and becomes monitor for his class, class four. He and his father are looking to see if his father will also win in his elections.

Angeline is now in class five. When the school year come to a close, she will take an end-of-year examination to determine at what level she will enter high school, and she will graduate from primary school.

The three children help their father prepare speeches, and they listen to him on the radio and give him feedback.

It is the week before the national elections, and Jacob still has not discussed his election campaign with Susan. On one particular night, he is giving a speech at a campaign rally near their home, and Susan leaves the children at home studying to attend the rally.

A few moments after she arrives, two members of the ruling party's election committee approach her and start talking to her. They say this is not Jacob's time. They say that they told Jacob not to run against the incumbent. The incumbent is an old man who has served faithfully for many terms. They say that, out of respect for his age and gratitude for his years of service, they want to give the incumbent his final term in office. Then, in the next election, the seat will be Jacob's.

The party members chat with Susan for a while, and then Susan is ready to go home. Jacob is about to speak, but she cannot stay to hear him. She decides that she will vote for him anyway. He is her husband, and many of the members of government were living the same kind of life of low moral conduct or had lived it in their younger days and had a broken family to show for it. She hopes to catch the older children before they fall asleep.

When she arrives home, Stephen is asleep, and Nicholas and Angeline are in bed. Nicholas is reading a novel in bed. He loves to do that, and sometimes to hide, he uses a flashlight. But Susan doesn't allow him to read late into the night, when school is in session. She insists that he must get enough sleep for school the next day. Sunday afternoon is reserved for reading. Susan has many developmental books and books on family matters for the children to read. Or they are allowed to read something of their choice. Also, during school holidays, Nicholas can read late in bed if he chooses.

On elections day, Jacob is discovered to be engaged, with the help of his mother and his older sisters, in some irregular practices to gain votes. Susan is surprised at how he doesn't seem to feel embarrassed; she is very embarrassed. Jacob and the incumbent are the only two candidates for the seat. In the end, Jacob loses the seat to the incumbent.

After the elections, friends of Susan tell her that Jacob had different women around with him during his campaigning. The electorate rejected him at the polls, saying, if that is what he does to his wife and children, what then will he do to the people?

Jacob runs in another three elections. Each time, he excludes his family. And each time, his number of votes decreases. He then ceases to run and gives up his dream of being a politician and becoming prime minister.

Soon after the elections are over and the new government is sworn in, the country is hit by a hurricane. The weather forecast says that Hurricane Hurley is scheduled to hit at a category-4 strength.

At first, Hurley was not a threat to Susan's island, but suddenly the storm makes a turn and is now expected to hit in three days in the night. Susan stocks up on canned foodstuff. She gets meats, fruits, vegetables, and biscuits and crackers, along with lots of juice and water. The children love canned sausages, so Susan buys a lot of those and lots of sardines for herself, but she does also buy other canned meats. She does not know exactly what to expect; it is the first hurricane she is going to experience. She has some excitement and anticipation for a first-time event. She also has some fear because of the scenes and reports she has seen and heard on television with respect to hurricanes--reports of destruction and even deaths.

She wonders if their home is going to withstand the onslaught. She knows that a storm designated as category 4 hits hard. She encourages the children to say a prayer to God every time they have a feeling of fear about what is going to happen. At nights when they are ready for bed, she kneels with the three of them by the bedside, and they pray to God for protection of their home and their lives. She wishes that the hurricane will make another sudden turn away from her island, and she prays for the safety of the islands that will be hit and of their peoples.

By the time Jacob arrives home (Susan didn't know whether or not he would) the electricity is already gone out. He had to take care of all his property and see to it that the buildings, which are all on the water's edge, are protected against high winds and the roofs are strong and sound to withstand the heavy rains that are expected. Although there are some lanterns in the home, Jacob arrives with flashlights for everyone, lots of batteries for the flashlights and the radio, and large jugs of water.

The winds already became very heavy earlier, and the electric company has turned off all the electricity throughout the island. Everywhere is dark, and Susan and the children are locked up tight inside. There can be no more cell phone conversations with friends in the neighborhood or across the island to compare notes, as the batteries have run low, and there is no means of recharging them. So Susan feels joy and relief when she sees that Jacob has come home.

Luckily for them, theirs is a gas stove. So Susan heats water, and everyone gets ready for bed. They all settle down in the parents' bed and are listening to the radio. The winds have become very fierce, and it has started to rain heavily. The community services are pleading with people to stay off the streets and remain indoors and not make things difficult for the fire and rescue forces and the hospital. Power lines have fallen, and debris is blowing wildly. Several sightseers have had to be rescued, and water is rising in many places. The radio station has lost a part of its roof, but commentators are still at work and giving full coverage of the hurricane. It is now midnight, and the radio commentators are giving news about houses loosing roofs, trees being uprooted, and rescue workers taking families to hurricane shelters.

The next thing Susan knows is that it is daylight. She is the first of the Wells family to awaken. The radio is silent, and she wonders if the batteries died. Everywhere is silent. The storm has passed. The family felt so secure with all the members huddled together that they all slept through the storm.

Susan opens the front door and sees debris in the yard. The ground is wet, and there are puddles of water here and there. She looks at Jacob's watch. It is eight thirty. Sunshine is peeping into the house through the corners of the curtains. She is hungry, so she has her breakfast of crackers and sardines with juice.

The children awaken one by one, and then Jacob wakes up. Those who have just woken look through the door, and then they all go out onto the porch. The view is amazing. Leaves and sticks and debris fill the entire yard and street. Small trees and shrubs are uprooted and lying on the ground. The asphalt from the road is lifted and lying in pieces on the sidewalks. The road is full of large potholes, and there are electric wires lying all over the ground. They are dead wires at least, because electricity is off throughout the whole island. Light poles are leaning over with transformers hanging on the side of them, and the scene is one of devastation. Thank God, though, that there are not any animals lying around.

Jacob and the children get breakfast for themselves. It is just so comforting to have the family all together. But immediately after breakfast, Jacob has to go into the capital to see how his business has fared. Susan and the children want to accompany him to do some sightseeing, but he says it is not the time for idleness and for sightseeing.

Shortly after he leaves, the radio comes back on, so Susan and the children get to hear news about what's going on around the island. The station's receiving pole got damaged by the heavy winds, and the station went off the air at 3:30 a.m. Now, at 2:00 p.m., it has just finished repairs and is able to restart transmitting. There have been no deaths, but many families had to be rescued from their homes when they lost their roofs and were taken to shelters during the night.

Now the sun is shining. It is a beautiful day, but it's not the beautiful island its residents are accustomed to seeing. The public works department has started to clear debris and remove fallen trees from the roads. The water in the gutters from the vantage point of the Wells gateway has subsided substantially, and a few cars are making their way cautiously along the road. The radio report says the estimated damage from the hurricane is $900,000. Although a category 4 hurricane was expected, by the time it hit the island, it was a category 3. There was not too much flooding, and most of the damage done was caused by the wind. Therefore many buildings lost their roofs.

As soon as the hurricane season is over in November, Jacob breaks ground on his residential property to build the family home. The plan has already been finalized, and it is a large two-story house on a small hill seven miles east of the capital. It is a five-bedroom, four and a half-bathroom house. The guest bedroom and private bath are on the first floor, along with the kitchen, dining, living, and family rooms and the half bathroom. Upstairs, there are four bedrooms and three bathrooms, plus a kitchenette and laundry room. Jacob tells Susan and the children that Christmas of the following year will see them settled in their new home. So Susan decides to make their last Christmas in their present home a memorable one.

The Christmas season comes. Stephen is in class one, Nicholas is in class four, and Angeline is in class five. She will graduate the following summer and go to high school. Angeline is now eleven, Nicholas is nine, and Stephen is six. Susan decides to have a big birthday celebration for all the children. Both Angeline and Jacob's birthdays are in December, and all the birthdays are within the last few months of the year. Susan's birthday is in October. The boys' are in September and October. Since the family will go to Puerto Rico before Christmas, Susan decides to have the celebration on December 30. The children can invite all their friends, and Susan will invite some adult friends of the family and a few neighbors. The party will be catered, and there will be rented bumper cars for the children and a disc jockey and dancing for everyone.

On December 30, they wake up to a heavy shower of rain in the morning. Everyone is worried about what the day will be like and how their party will fare. But by midday, the sun comes out. By evening, it has dried up the ground and makes fine weather for a party.

The children arrive by four o'clock and are delightfully surprised when they see the bumper cars. They are not interested in the food and spend two hours having fun in the bumper cars until Susan calls them to come out and eat something. Susan extends the rental of the bumper cars and tells them that whoever's parents will bring them back, they can come the next day and New Year's Day and use the cars with Angeline and her brothers.

Many of the children do come back, and the Wells children have a fun time until New Year's Day.

Chapter

A LEADING MALE ROLE MODEL

There is a lawyer who lives and practices in the city about whom you have already heard. His name is Robert Aldrin. The community looks up to him and thinks that he has the answers to many of their questions and the solutions to their problems. People invite him to speak at many functions. Even the ladies organizations invite him to give lectures. Robert is a short, unimpressive man who is bald in the front. He has piercing brown eyes and a well-built nose, and he talks very rapidly. He seems to be in a successful marriage with a stable family, unlike many of the leading politicians. He is a very expensive lawyer, but he wins most of his cases. He handles mostly criminal defense cases, representing busted drug dealers and defendants in large robbery cases.

Because of all this and because Robert is an outstanding member of the local men's club, Susan herself thought he was a good masculine role model. This was why she went to him early in her marriage when she discovered that Jacob was being unfaithful, hoping that he could be a powerful mediator or a great lawyer.

The first question Susan asked him after she greeted him in his office was, "Do you think you can work against the interest of Jacob Wells in the event things should come to that?"

Robert called his secretary and asked her to check the files. Then he said to Susan, "Jacob Wells is not a client of mine."

Robert offered Susan a seat and listened to all she had to say. She told him about the role Jacob's mother was playing in their marriage and how Adassa had encouraged Jacob into unfaithfulness. She told him that, if the marriage could be saved, she would rather have that than divorce. As Jacob's taunting reaction to the meeting made clear, Robert did not follow through on his promises to Susan.

Susan had another experience with Robert one evening when she attended a ladies group lecture. She'd heard the lecture advertised on the radio and learned that Robert Aldrin was to be the guest speaker. She did not appreciate the trend of his speech, which sounded quite disempowering to women and generally of a low moral standard.

Eventually, as a great shock to Susan, she heard Robert say, "A man can plant his seed wherever he pleases as long as he turns back and waters it."

At this point, she got up and left the meeting. She has always wondered if the women had given him applause at the end of his speech.

Susan now knows that Robert is not a good male role model. She hears his voice often on the radio, with excerpts from his lectures and speeches and is often disgusted at the low moral level of what he has to say. The government is now proposing to constitute a Bill of Rights for the country and is considering new laws governing illegitimate children and people in "committed relationship," (couples who are cohabitating). The aim is to dispense with the word *illegitimate* and to give more rights to illegitimate children so that illegitimate children who are born to husbands outside of their marriages can have rights to inheritance.

The government opens the discussion to the public. One morning, Susan hears Robert on the radio. He says that more rights for illegitimate children will not affect the family.

It is two days before she goes on summer vacation with the children to Canada, and she doesn't have time for a full commentary examining all the details of the matter. But she feels she must challenge his point about more rights for illegitimate children not affecting the family. She is brief and direct in a letter to the editor. It states:

Dear Madam:

I heard excerpts of the reputable Mr. Robert Aldrin's speech concerning constitutional changes in our country and took particular note of his concerns regarding the rights of illegitimate children. I really do not have the time to go into details about different aspects of the argument, but I must challenge his point that giving more rights to illegitimate children will not affect the family. Does Mr. Aldrin wish to tell me that certain women in this community can suddenly decide that it is now profitable for them to have some Wells children under the proposed new law and it wouldn't affect me and my three children? Of course it may not affect the men at the heads of the families; because those who are callous enough to do the things that some of them are doing cannot be affected by anything, least of all the feelings of women and children.

In brief, Mr. Aldrin, I must tell you that illegitimate children, by whatever name they may be called or not called, do affect the family. This effect is not only financial, but also mental, emotional, and otherwise. And evidently, such must affect the nation in the long run.

Does Mr. Aldrin have facts and statistics to show that such constitutional changes did not adversely affect other countries in the Caribbean before he encourages our nation to follow other nations blindly and make the same pitfalls?

I would like the lawmaking body to understand that, contrary to what Mr. Aldrin thinks, such decisions must affect the family and the nation eventually.

Very sincerely,
Susan Wells

On returning from vacation, Susan notices that there is silence on the proposed Bill of Rights. She is listening and reading carefully so she can pick up where she left off. She believes that it is the creation of such Bills of Rights that has caused degeneration in the family structure. Of course life is not perfect, and people are not perfect, and there have been illegitimate children along the way. There has even been cohabitation in some instances. However, when governing bodies create laws to protect and encourage such deviation from intact family structure, it fosters irresponsibility in individuals prone to irresponsibility. Susan feels that such laws have led to the indiscipline that is seen in the schools.

She believes that cohabitation is no form of committed relationship and that the only committed relationship is marriage. However, people must distinguish between a marriage and a wedding. Marriage is all about commitment—that's what it is, making a commitment to each other. The wedding is the ceremony in which the couple and minister perform the rites. She feels that society should teach responsibility, rather than protect and reward irresponsibility.

Finally, there is more talk of the proposed Bill of Rights. Then one morning on the radio news, she again hears Robert Aldrin. He says that, with every right, there is a responsibility. What he doesn't say is that adults are called upon to be responsible parents and stop creating illegitimate children if they don't like the consequences.

Susan is sarcastic in the title she gives to her next commentary, and she writes again for the newspaper. She writes:

Illegitimacy without a Name?
By Susan Wells

The talk of the proposed Bill of Rights in respect to illegitimate offspring has surfaced again. One renowned male voice that has been agitating for increased legal rights for illegitimate children has finally made his own concluding statement. "With every right, there is a responsibility," he says. However, he has not mentioned any proposed responsibilities.

With regard to illegitimacy, I do not see that children are being robbed of their birthright. I see that they duly inherit what their parents have bequeathed them—some illegitimacy and others legitimacy. If, therefore, illegitimacy is such a big taboo, how is it that so many parents choose it for their children?

What I do see is that humans are being robbed of their dignity when male voices like the one mentioned above continue to communicate to men that they "can plant their seed wherever they please" (thus abusing women), "as long as they turn back and water it" (thus severing the final threads of dignity of the legitimate family where the man has a wife with children). Children inherit a lot more than material things. In fact, life is about a lot more than material possessions. And just as offspring inherit material possessions, they inherit genes and habits and other traits, as well as the results of their parents' many choices and actions.

So do we really need legal protection of rights then? Or do we need the teaching of responsibility? Wouldn't all children inherit normally if their mothers were thinking, *My child will inherit as long as I am responsible enough not to entertain, encourage, aid, and abet another woman's husband in my bed*? And wouldn't this be the case, too, if their fathers were thinking responsibly, *My child will duly inherit as long as I am not sneaking around corners and in the dark or tiptoeing out of my home in the middle of the night when I believe that my wife and children are asleep?*

If one argues that illegitimate children should not be held responsible for their parents' actions then one refutes the whole theory of inheritance. If children should not inherit fruitless bequests of their parents, then there is no strong argument that they should inherit fruitful bequests. If any aspect of the Bill of Rights should be established on unbalanced judgment without logical reasoning, then what would eventually become of the society?

We have already seen the degeneration in the more advanced societies. Is this the direction in which our nation wishes to go? It seems as though leaders of nations have long been manipulating laws to accommodate their own immorality. From where did countries receive their laws governing murder and stealing? There is where lawmakers should go to find other laws. Why are there no sound laws governing adultery? Adultery is fraud. Why would we want laws to protect and reward it? How will new laws in favor of illegitimate children affect legitimate children and the legitimate family? Some men say there will be no effect, while others never thought about it. How many have asked women and children?

Will there be clauses in the new laws to protect against abuse of the new rights? Here some women on the streets can just say, "It is now profitable for me to have a child or some children for such and such a married man. That will be my form of income and inheritance.

Just what are we saying here? Do we feel that legitimate children should be punished for their legitimacy and that there are wives who should be punished for bearing children within wedlock? At what point does a nation decide that right should be punished and wrong rewarded? What is right and what is wrong in our nation?

I can assure my readers that the laws of the Bible are right for any Christian nation. They are the foundation of an orderly and lawful society. "But we must distinguish between the laws of the Bible and the practices during Bible times of men and women exactly like those of today."

> *"But we must distinguish between the laws of the Bible and the practices during Bible times of men and women exactly like those of today."*

I wish to know how it is that so many modern day adults can get away with seeing the world through one eye while they admonish the youth to charge forward with both eyes closed. Leaders of communities would be far more constructive to advise their followers to become responsible citizens and, further, responsible, rather than irresponsible, parents.

Parents should make a stable home for their offspring. They should providing training, disciplining, and nurturing, instead of being preoccupied, as is suggested by the aforementioned leading male voice, with grabbing for material possessions and with taking steps to steal what already belong to others. Or are we moving toward becoming lower than the other animals?

What we, as a Christian nation, really need to do for our children is to clearly point them to the parts of the Word of God that teach about marriage and family. We must punish unfaithfulness and reestablish a stable family structure to be headed by responsible and accountable parents. The rest of society will fall automatically into place, and our children will love, thank, and respect us for it.

Chapter 10

SOME IMPORTANT OCCURRENCES

It was summer 1990 when Susan and the children spent their vacation in Canada. Stephen was still in kindergarten, and Nicholas and Angeline were still in primary school. The year had been progressing quite uneventfully, except for the children's usual high test scores. Susan had decided during their Easter holidays that, in the summer, the children would visit Canada to meet their maternal side of the family. Susan has a large family in Canada, some of whom the children had already met in the Caribbean. However, they had been very small at the time and would not remember these family members at their present age. She knew that the children were now at an age when they would know their relatives and appreciate the experience of a foreign culture.

The children have their maternal grandmother and their grandmother's sister, two aunts and two uncles and their families, and second cousins too (the children of their grandaunt). They arrived in Toronto, Canada, just in time for the annual family picnic. Susan had the pleasure of seeing the children interact with their relatives and have fun with their cousins, who were mostly in their own age range. But most pleasurable was seeing Nicholas identify with the men's group and join in the rough games. The men of the family were good male role models for both boys. The uncles tried to engage Stephen in whatever games he could manage. Angeline frolicked about with the girls and engaged in conversation with aunts and aunts-in-law.

Of all the sites and attractions, the children visited they loved mostly the Science Center. There they not only enjoyed the exhibits and experiments but were also able to engage in a large variety of activities and perform experiments of their own. Apart from visiting the homes of the different families, Angeline and Nicholas revisited some of the sites and spent many hours at the Science Center with cousins of their own age and older. The children were sad to leave Canada and, on their return home, asked Susan to move the family to live in Canada. That was not an option for Susan, as she was not going to remove the children from their father.

It is now, however, 1992, and Easter has arrived. The construction of the Wells's house has not progressed as expected. The anticipated funds are not being realized. Jacob's finances have started to decline, as his businesses have been declining. He has leased the first and the second phases, the restaurant complex and the marina. But he still has the construction company, a car rental, and a real estate business, none of which are thriving as they used to do. The house will be completed but maybe at a slower pace than planned.

The businesses under Jacob's management are not thriving because they are not very well run. Whereas Jacob is very good at establishing a business—and he has opened many well-planned businesses that have been well needed in the community and well received by the people—and he would be a good director, he is not a good manager. He readily gains many loyal customers but eventually loses them, as he doesn't continue to deliver reliable service. His employees are not well supervised, and all his earnings are not directed into his accounts. He is not a good manager of people, time, or money. Instead of hiring competent managers for the different businesses and supervising those managers carefully, he insists on running all the establishments himself. He does not even ask Susan to help with anything, so Susan doesn't even know who the businesses belong to.

SOME IMPORTANT OCCURRENCES

Susan warns the children to pay attention in school and to get themselves a good education. She says they must not rest their hopes on what they see their father has and whether or not he is successful.

In May, Angeline sits for her final examinations in primary school to determine at what academic level she will enter high school. The exam consists of three papers, namely language (and the nation's official language is English), mathematics, and social studies. Pupils are graded A, B, or C on each paper, A being the highest score and C the lowest.

The highest academic performance is to obtain three A's. Angeline feels confident in all her subjects, and all her class test scores are excellent. She writes the examinations and feels satisfied with her performance. May ends and the family waits to see the results.

When June arrives, the family learns that Angeline has gotten three A's. What excitement! Susan tells the children that, to celebrate Angeline's achievement, she will take them to Canada for Christmas vacation so they can see snow. June comes to a close, and the Wells family receives even more good news. Not only does Angeline achieve the highest academic score, but she is also named Class Student of the Year. This means she has been considered by her class teacher to be the highest achiever in all aspects of school life and the best all-around student in her class.

Angeline graduates from primary school on the honor roll and with the other aforementioned accomplishments. At graduation, she wears a sash that reads, "1992 Class Student of the Year," and receives a large trophy saying the same. That is only one of the five trophies she receives on graduating from primary school.

Nicholas and Stephen are also on the honor roll at the end of the school year. They each receive a trophy that reads, "1992 Honor Roll," as well as several certificates for high achievement in various academic areas and other important aspects of school life. For example, Stephen receives another certificate for being the most loving student in his class.

The children spend the summer holidays at home with Carol, engaging in their favorite activities and games, watching television, and enjoying the freedom from daily studying and homework. However, Susan goes over all their test papers for the term, and they correct anything they got wrong. This she has been doing every holiday since they entered primary school, and it only takes a day or two. During the week, Carol teaches them little tasks like tidying their rooms and arranging their clothes in the drawers. On the weekends, Susan takes them to the beach and to appropriate movies. Not too much is seen of Jacob. But when he is around on the weekend, the children jump on him in the bed and make him get up to play board games and card games with them.

September comes, and Angeline starts high school in class with all the students of her own age with the highest academic achievement. Nicholas goes to class five, where he now has to prepare for final exams the following calendar year. Stephen goes to class one, starting his second of six years in primary school. Susan is touched to see how far the family has advanced and how intelligent and ambitious the children are.

She is also shocked to see that all these accomplishments do not impress Jacob to the point where he wants to improve himself and elevate his standard of living. He is not even motivated to do so for the sake of respect for the children, now that they are getting old enough to understand and experience the embarrassment that their mother already experiences. Now they are heading into high school, Susan is prepared for when they come home and tell her what the children have to say to them about where they see their father. She will have to comfort them and teach them how to deal with cruel idiots. But in the highest academic environment, they will have a milder experience than they might otherwise have had.

In class five, it becomes obvious that Nicholas doesn't like language as much as his other subjects. He begins to struggle with it. So Susan decides that some extra language lessons during the Christmas holidays will be the solution to that problem.

However, this solution creates another problem—namely, how does she support Nicholas without punishing Angeline by not fulfilling the promise of Christmas vacation in Canada and the experience of winter and snow?

The ultimate solution comes readily to Susan. She decides that Angeline will go by herself to Canada for Christmas. All the plans are made. December comes, and as soon as school closes, Angeline is off to Canada, laden with gifts for all the family. There will be the annual Christmas gathering, and gifts will be exchanged. Susan makes sure that Angeline is prepared.

Susan did not have to prepare winter clothes for Angeline. Those will be provided by the family in Canada. So she made all the arrangements with the airline for Angeline to travel as an unaccompanied minor and to be met at the Toronto airport by her grandmother. Meanwhile, she arranges for Nicholas to spend some of his Christmas holidays attending private lessons in English language with his class teacher.

She tries to make Christmas at home lively for herself and the boys, as they all feel some loneliness with Angeline gone. Jacob takes them for one day to Puerto Rico so the boys can buy Christmas presents. Everyone buys a gift for Angeline. Susan bakes fruitcakes and makes sorrel and ginger beer and prepares special dinners, and she and the boys go to midnight Mass for Christmas and New Year.

It is an earful of excited stories when Angeline returns home in the New Year just in time for the start of her second term in high school. She brings gifts for everyone and happily opens all her gifts the day after her return. The following day she will return to school, whereas the boys already started the new term.

May 1993 arrives, and Nicholas must have been feeling some insecurities and estimating what his results may be in the final examinations because he asks Susan, "If I do not get three A's, will I be able to go to Canada for Christmas?"

After a quick thought and Susan reasoning that he will be doing his best as usual and his accomplishment will not be far from three A's, she says, "Yes. Of course."

He seems to breathe a sigh of relief. Susan knows that her response is only a just and fair one; it can only build confidence in him, letting him know that his best will be good enough to be rewarded. Moreover, at this time Nicholas still sees his sister as his role model and makes every effort to follow in his older sibling's footsteps. So it was then and there established as a family tradition that, when a child moves on to high school, he or she goes to Canada for Christmas to experience winter and snow.

By the middle of June, all the wait and wondering is over. Nicholas gets a B for language. He obtains A's for both mathematics and social studies. So his score is BAA. At graduation, he is on the honor roll and receives a trophy for that, along with three other trophies, one of which is a trophy for outstanding contribution in soccer. He also receives many certificates for outstanding performance in the various academic and social areas. He is satisfied, and his family is proud of him.

Stephen is also on the honor roll and receives the honor roll trophy and many certificates for outstanding performance in all academic and social disciplines.

Angeline receives an outstanding report, with all A's and A+'s for all three terms in first form.

The BAA score lands Nicholas in the top academic group in high school. Christmas comes, and off he goes to Canada, laden with gifts for the Christmas party. Just like Angeline, he travels as an unaccompanied minor to be met in Canada by his grandmother, who will meet him at the airport with a winter coat.

It is another lonely Christmas for Susan and the two children left behind, and Susan makes sure that they do all their usual Christmas traditions. Those at home spend one day in Puerto Rico, just like they had during the year before, to buy gifts for all the children. Angeline asks her father to buy extra decorations to decorate the yard as well as the house. Susan bakes fruitcakes and makes sorrel and ginger beer. She prepares sumptuous dinners for the weekends and for Christmas and New Year's. And Susan and the children go to the midnight Masses.

Another Christmas passes without them being in their new home. But by the look of things, they should move in for next Christmas.

Nicholas returns just in time for the start of school in January with his excited stories and gifts for everyone. He is happy to open all his gifts and to admire the decorated outdoors, but he is more anxious to return to school and share his experience with his classmates and friends.

January does not end before Susan begins to hear exciting news on the radio. This is international news. Somewhere in the Western world, a woman had cut off her husband's penis and was eventually acquitted in court. With all the excitement at home, Susan had missed all the details, but the crime and the acquittal of the offender was enough to stimulate all of Susan's senses and her affinity to commenting. She immediately writes a letter to the editor of the only newspaper that she thinks will publish it. Why? Because this editor is a woman. She writes:

Dear Madam:

I am so happy to hear that the woman who cut off her husband's penis was recently acquitted. That a jury could rule in the woman's favor tells us that the wider community and the leaders of communities are understanding the kind of criminal emotional abuse system under which many women live for many, many years for one reason or another. This is not to mention the physical, financial, and other criminal abuse many women endure.

In the past, and still in the present, we see open injustice to women because men and women are judged by the community at large based on double moral standards. Some women have so helplessly accepted this discrepancy that they train their own children accordingly.

What are men reaping from all this? Isn't it obvious that there is a greater number of male dropouts from society than there are female dropouts? Isn't it so that males are mostly the ones involved in illegal drug abuse, whether by addiction or by trade?

I have long thought that many a man needed to lose this precious gift of God, his penis, as he showed by his lifestyle that he was unaware of how to use it. As I am not a supporter of a return to the days of barbarism, I pray that education, enlightenment, and understanding may bring justice to our world—justice toward women especially.

And, by the way, in Ann Landers's newspaper column late last year, the story was told of a young man who wore a T-shirt saying, "Help stamp out virginity." For me the story went well until the point at which the young man was then the father of a young girl going out on her first date. I think the story should have ended that the man would wear the T-shirt as he met his daughter's first escort at the door. I hope the message is clear.

Thank you.

Sincerely,
Susan Wells

Ever since Susan's case in the magistrate's court and the subsequent changing of the law, Susan has been reading in the newspaper and hearing on the radio about the various domestic violence cases that are tried in the magistrate's court. Of course, most of them are about wife battering. Sadly though, most of the cases are being thrown out before they are tried, or the husbands are being acquitted of any wrong-doing, for one reason or another. Robert Aldrin is representing all the men. There are no female lawyers in the community, and so the wives are being represented by males.

Susan is infuriated by the way the matter is progressing, until one day she reads of a wife battering case that is proceeding to the High Court of Justice because the husband pleaded not guilty. The wife hired a female lawyer from another Caribbean island, in order to have the best representation.

Robert Aldrin is once again the defense lawyer, and Susan follows the case in the newspaper. In the High Court, the husband is found guilty. Before Easter, on March 7, the outcome of the case is reported in the newspapers. Now the following day, March 8, the community is set to celebrate International Women's Day.

Susan decides to contribute to the celebrations with the following newspaper commentary.

Stop the Violence
By Susan Wells

As far as I am concerned, we here in our little island celebrated International Women's Day in true local fashion. Regretfully, the incident that makes me come to this conclusion did not occur on the exact day, March 8, but on the previous day, March 7. However, it is close enough, and we will have to be satisfied with the reality.

I can assure this community that many women were heartened to hear the result of a case of woman battering by the husband of the complainant, which was recently tried in the High Court and reported on the day before International Women's Day. It was interesting to note that the man first pleaded innocent. I am sure that was an attempt to beat the system, which he had learned over the years was going to support him. It was rather exciting, on the other hand, to note that when "fire was set at his tail," he changed his plea to tell the truth.

Encouraging was the judge's response of scolding; fining; and, most importantly, directing the convicted to seek to improve himself. Men who are now feeling very frightened (whether you wear neckties or overalls, shirt-jacs or suits, and who know that the honorable judge was also speaking to you), the important message here is to seek to improve yourselves. Again the operative word is *seek*. As our scripture says, "Seek and you shall find" (Luke 11:9).

In this year, 1994, which is designated "International Year of the Family," any nation that truly seeks solutions to its many social problems will find what modern terminology will want to refer to as family-friendly laws.

The next three months pass uneventfully. Then it is the end of another academic year. All three children successfully complete another stage of their education, with the usual academic excellence. At the end of her second year in high school, Angeline has distinguished herself among the top three in her class. She and Nicholas receive reports of A's and A+'s in all their subjects, while Stephen is again on the honor roll in class two.

They all spend a quiet and relaxing summer. They spend the weekdays at home with Carol, and on the weekends, they go to the beach with Susan or to the swimming pool and restaurant for lunch. On Sundays, they go with Susan to church and sometimes to the site to see how the house is progressing.

At the end of summer Jacob tells the family that the house will be ready by the end of October. They will be able to move in any time in November, so they will be settled in for Christmas.

The Wells moved into a four-bedroom, two-bathroom house shortly after Stephen was born, and Angeline had her own room while the boys shared one bedroom. Now they will move into a five-bedroom home, where each of the children will have his or her own room—his or her own home. Jacob and Susan will share a large twin bedroom and bath, with twin clothes closets, twin washbasins, and twin beds. Susan will mostly occupy the room, since Jacob does not spend much time at home.

Susan and the children start sorting and packing on the weekends and going often to see if the house is really going to be ready this time for Christmas. Their anticipation and excitement also start growing.

Finally it is December 1, and 97 Lincoln Avenue, Everson Park, is the address of the Wells family. Susan has invited a few of her friends, and the children have invited a few of their friends, all from church. The priest is asked to come and bless the home. After the blessing, there is a cocktail party to end the evening.

As soon as school closes in December, the family goes to Puerto Rico for a long weekend, Friday to Monday. There, they complete a fairly large shopping venture, picking out new furniture and accessories to put the finishing touches on their new home. Jacob allows Stephen to buy a few video games, but the older children choose things that they want to finish their rooms. Jacob buys them a computer to complete the office furnishings.

The weekend after their return home, Susan bakes the fruitcakes and puts them to soak in wine and makes the sorrel and ginger beer. She helps the children immediately afterward to tidy and arrange their rooms. Every evening after work, she puts the finishing touches on the rest of the house, with all the new curtains and dressings.

When Susan is gone to work, Angeline and her brothers put up Christmas lights and decorations and decorate the Christmas tree. Carol seasons the turkey. On Christmas Eve, Susan will set the dining table with the special dinnerware that they use for special holidays. She will cover the set table with a mesh fabric to protect it from dust. With all the new things to buy for the house, they didn't bother with decorations for the garden, but they decided that decorating the garden would be a part of their Christmas tradition in years to come.

Chapter 11

THE CHILDREN PERFORM

Dancing has taken an upward turn for Susan. The National Tourist Board has asked her dance group, along with two other cultural groups in the country, to accompany them on a three-week tour overseas to promote their country as a tourist destination. The country wants to highlight itself in Germany, France, Norway, and Sweden and has planned activities in the capital cities of all these nations. The tour will take place the last two weeks in April and the first week in May. The leader of the group likes Susan and wants her to make the trip. But Susan has to think about whether or not she wants to leave the children for such a long time.

She thinks hard about the matter and reasons that the children sometimes take her for granted since she is with them all the time. They sometimes pay more respect to their father because they rarely spend quality time with him. She decides to take the tour and leave the children in the care of their father. Carol will look after the home as usual during the day and be with them until six thirty in the evenings after school. They know and love Carol, and Carol loves them too. Ever since Stephen started primary school and attending all day instead of half day, Carol has had flexible hours. When school is in session, she can come at midday and work until six thirty in the evenings. During holidays, she comes early. Susan comes home as early as possible. Now when Susan is gone, she will work from midday until six thirty in the evening. Jacob will have some responsibility to get the children out to school in the mornings and take care of them in the nights and on weekends.

Susan talks with the children about all this and reminds them that it is important that they continue in the same disciplined way that they are accustomed to and pay full attention to their lessons. She will be back at the end of three weeks, and she will bring them presents from all the different countries.

For a whole month before the departure, the dance group meets four weeknights, Monday to Thursday, to sew new costumes. Susan leaves the children from eight o'clock when Stephen is in bed until quarter to ten before Angeline goes to bed.

The middle of April comes, and off she goes for a little time for herself.

Jacob doesn't seem pleased and looks at her with angry eyes when she returns home. But she knows he doesn't dare hit her because she will just take him to court. The penalty has gotten much stiffer for the convicted over time as the domestic violence continues. More than that, Angeline tells Susan that, when they went to bed at nights, their father left until the following morning, when he returned to take them to school. Susan just comforts all three of the children and promises that she will never leave them for so long again until they have all graduated from high school.

Now that Susan has returned home from her tour, Jacob does not come home on a regular basis. He stays away for days at a time.

Susan doesn't trouble her head about him. The time she just had to herself was truly exhilarating and will certainly nourish her until Stephen graduates from high school. As long as the children are maturing responsibly and healthily in all aspects of their being, she is satisfied and encouraged to plod on.

Just so, summer comes. Angeline and Nicholas are playing in their school band for end-of-year activities. Two years ago, Angeline joined the school band and played for graduation after her first year in the band. Nicholas joined last year and is now playing for graduation along with his sister for the first time. All three children end the school year in their usual academic excellence—Angeline and Nicholas with only A's and A+'s -on their report cards and Stephen on the honor roll, with many certificates for specific social and academic achievements. That is Susan's sustenance to carry on.

Now that Angeline and Nicholas are established in the school band, they go to school on Saturday mornings for practice. On Saturday afternoons, they go to church for advanced catechumen lessons. So Susan and Stephen go to the beach most Saturday mornings.

One particular Saturday, Susan and Stephen are on the beach. Susan is enjoying the fresh sea air as usual when she is suddenly distressed by the smell of cigarette smoke. At first she cannot tell from which direction the smoke is coming. She just wonders why someone would want to come out to pollute such a pleasant atmosphere. She keeps looking around and sniffing. Eventually she spots a gentleman who is smoking. He sees the disapproval on her face. In response, he makes himself prominent and confidently blows out a large puff of smoke in her direction. As she struggles to breathe, the man boldly shows off his confidence and satisfaction in his freedom to please himself with his smoking and puffing. Susan doesn't want to give him the added pleasure of displacing her by moving from her spot, but she thinks how grossly unfair it is that she is forced to inhale his puffs, especially since it is a rather unhealthy thing for all human beings.

In a few days, she has a letter written to the editor, which reads as follows:

Dear Madam:

Now that our new government has been duly formed and we anticipate attention soon to be turned to the finalization of our new Constitution, and ultimately our first Bill of Rights, I would like to bring to the attention of our lawmakers the right of nonsmokers not to smoke.

I am sure that even smokers would recognize this right. To the best of my knowledge, our nation was never what one would consider to be a smoking community. Yet some people do smoke. Although doctors have said that smoking is very bad for our health, it is seen that many people wish to reserve their right to smoke. On the other hand, nonsmokers also wish to reserve their right not to smoke—that is, the fumes of the smokers' cigarettes.

I know many doctors have advised their smoking patients that, in the best interest of personal health, they should at least exhale the smoke they puff rather than inhale it. However, I think it is just to say that those who feel they must smoke should, in the best interest of nonsmokers, be compelled to inhale their fumes. This, of course, does not fully alleviate the suffering of nonsmokers. Other measures that could be considered are strategically placed smoking booths like telephone booths (fully enclosed though) and laws compelling smokers to exercise their right only in the confines of those booths, their homes, or their hotel rooms.

I would like to point here to a closed feature aired on a regular morning show of our local radio station on April 13, 1994. The feature entitled "How to Have Younger-Looking Skin," noted one solution was to stop smoking if you are a smoker. But we are all smokers. The only difference is that some would like to stop while others wish to continue.

On page 20 of the April 30, 1994, issue of a local newspaper, a columnist doctor's piece addressed the issue of smoking. A letter writer stated that his father had stopped smoking and his high blood pressure had stabilized, to the extent that he was being weaned from his high blood pressure medication. There are these and other reported personal benefits of not smoking. But when one thinks of a smoker who has children, is there any greater act of selfishness?

What impact would stringent measures have on our efforts to preserve the purity of our environment?

Yours sincerely,
Susan Wells

As the Wells family enters the final months of 1995, Angeline is a senior in high school and is scheduled to graduate in two years. At the end of the present year, she will be fifteen. Nicholas is in his final year of junior high school and will be thirteen by year's end. Stephen is also a senior but in primary school and is expected to start high school in two years. At year's end, he will be ten. It seems like so quickly they have grown from innocent, helpless little beings to be big responsible individuals. No more does Susan have to wonder what they will turn out to be. She knows, as she tells them often, that they can be anything they wish to be in this life.

December arrives, and school closes for the Christmas holidays. Jacob has not said anything about going to Puerto Rico. He continues to stay away for days at a time and come home at any time of the day or night. Carol says he comes by some days and checks the refrigerator and the cupboards and leaves with clothes.

Well, he comes the weekend before Christmas and takes the children grocery shopping and fills the refrigerator and all the cupboards. Then late in the night on Christmas Eve, he arrives laden with gifts for everyone, including several toys for Stephen. The children just place the gifts, unwrapped, among the already wrapped ones under the Christmas tree.

By this time, the house is all clean and decorated. Everything is ready for celebrating the holidays, and Susan and the children will soon get dressed to go to midnight Mass. This year, as all the children are quite mature now and can stay up late longer, they will also celebrate the pre-Christmas service caroling before the midnight Mass on Christmas Eve. They invite Jacob to join them for the services, but he is not interested.

The fruitcakes are baked and soaking in wine, and the ginger beer and sorrel are made. The Christmas tree is beautiful and lit and laden with presents underneath. The living room and the children's rooms and the garden are beautifully lit with Christmas lights, all decorated by Angeline and her brothers. The turkey is seasoned by Carol and resting in the refrigerator. The dining table is set and covered. The ham is cooked and ready for breakfast in the morning.

When Carol returns from holidays she will find her present under the Christmas tree. Susan is home for the week until after New Year's Day because her office still closes for that week. Carol will have New Year's Eve off because Susan will be home.

Susan and the children return home from church about half past one on Christmas morning and open some of their gifts before having a snack of fruitcake and sorrel and a few hours of sleep.

Susan awakes first and puts the turkey into the oven and then makes the usual Christmas breakfast of fried eggs and ham with buttered toasts and eggnog (this eggnog is without alcohol). The children awake and come downstairs one by one. All are down by the time breakfast is ready. They all eat together and then open the rest of their gifts and have a family time together without Jacob. His gifts and several others are left under the Christmas tree. There is Christmas music playing throughout the house as everyone relaxes and the children receive friends and talk on the phone.

Late afternoon, the turkey is already out of the oven. The children help Susan prepare the side dishes for dinner—rice and peas (pigeon peas), candied sweet potatoes, fried eggplant, and a tossed salad. They have dinner together and are spending a quiet evening at home when a call comes in from Jacob. He speaks with the children for a long while, after which the children tell Susan that he says Merry Christmas to her.

On Boxing Day, the children sleep late and everyone gets his or her breakfast on arising. This is a quiet, restful day when there is enough food cooked to satisfy the family for the day. The children enjoy their Christmas gifts, and Susan speaks on the telephone with her family in Canada. Late in the afternoon, Jacob comes by and behaves just as if he lives there. He opens up the fridge and gets himself a plate of food and serves himself some fruit cake and ginger beer, and the children all gather around him at the table and eat cake. Afterward, they get him to open up his gifts.

As he sits in the living room, Susan asks him, "Where do you live?"

"At 97 Lincoln Avenue, Everson Park," he says with a big grin on his face, having given the address of their home.

Susan is happy for the time he spends with them in the home, and she wonders what his problem is. Why does he not live the kind of life she would consider normal? But since he does not choose to have conversation with her, she just forgets the matter. When he leaves, she looks in his closet and finds that more than half of his clothes are missing. When Carol returns to work, she tells Susan that, while she and her husband were out late on Christmas night, they saw Jacob out with one of his women, Lowrine Scrapple, and he said hello to her.

The rest of Susan's holiday week passes in a restful, relaxed way, with two trips to the beach with the children. One day, she drives Angeline and Nicholas to the movies, where they meet with friends and enjoy a matinee, while Stephen chooses to stay home and enjoy his toys.

On New Year's Eve, they go again to caroling and midnight Mass and return at about half past one on New Year's Day. They eat and drink of the Christmas preparations before going to bed and sleeping late.

When they all awake and are downstairs, Susan makes the same breakfast they had at Christmas, with hot chocolate instead of eggnog. The children and their father speak on the phone, and they help Susan to make a sumptuous holiday dinner and dessert. At night, Susan and the children watch a movie at home before going to bed.

As the New Year becomes old, Susan and the children are settled at work and in school. They begin to see less and less of Jacob. Stephen begins to complain that his is a broken home and to be sad sometimes. The older children do not appear to be bothered. Susan just tries to comfort Stephen and to encourage him not to worry about things over which he has no control. She tells him he does not have anything to be ashamed about. He didn't do anything wrong. And she reminds all the children that a good education is the thing that will give them the ability to rise above the heartbreak of a broken home and help them correct the situation in their own lives. Thus, she tells them they should keep their minds on their lessons, which is their childhood career.

Carol says that Jacob continues to come home from time to time and examine the refrigerator and the cupboards and leave with clothes. She says that one of the days she asked him, "Why are you doing this to your family?"

"I love and take care of my family," he replied.

Jacob, though he continues to attend all the functions in which any of the children is involved as long as he isn't overseas, always arrives late and stands in the back of the room. At the end of the function, he takes pictures. Sometimes, the family goes out to dinner before Susan and the children drive home.

Susan has overcome all her anger, hurt, and resentments with the comforting words of scripture. "She finds that making friends with Jesus has provided her with an ever-present companion who is more than able to meet all her needs." So when the whole family is together, like at those dinners, it is a pleasant encounter.

> *"She finds that making friends with Jesus has provided her with an ever-present companion who is more than able to meet all her needs."*

Summer comes and the usual end-of-the-school-year activities take place. Angeline and Nicholas play in their school band at graduation exercises. All the children successfully complete the year's work and receive honorable mention and certificates for outstanding academic and social accomplishments.

The usual holiday activities take place, one of which is reviewing of end-of-term test papers and correcting all mistakes. Luckily for these children who pay attention throughout the term, this activity takes only a Saturday for each child. After this, they are all free to engage in their wealth of games and activities with which their father provides them. There are also the trips to the beach, when Susan is at home, and trips to the movies, sometimes now a night movie. There are now overseas church camps for Angeline and Nicholas that last sometimes as long as two weeks.

Now that the children are older and they don't see their father at home they have taken on a new activity of getting dressed on Saturday afternoons and taking the bus, all three of them, and going to visit their father at his office. He brings them home in the night, laden with groceries. Sometimes he stays for a while, and the whole family has a concert on the patio, each person performing except for Jacob, who only looks on in amazement. At these times, there is a lot of laughter. Or sometimes, they play cards or dominoes, and Susan wins a lot.

Summer ends, and Angeline starts her final year of high school. Nicholas starts his senior high school years, and Stephen starts his final year of primary education. At the end of the calendar year, Angeline will be sixteen, Nicholas will be fourteen, and Stephen will be eleven years old.

Chapter 12

TWO MAJOR MILESTONES OCCUR

The very first term of Stephen's final primary school year his test papers begin to show that he is struggling with social studies, and he says he does not like the subject. Susan sees that it is a similar case to his older brother's and convinces him that he needs some extra lessons to prepare for his final exams. He decides that he will do lessons during the Christmas holidays, and Susan immediately secures a place for him with his class teacher.

The end of the year—always a significant time because all the birthdays occur in the last few months and then the celebrations culminate in the Christmas tradition—comes around. In December, Angeline turns sixteen. Normally, birthdays are celebrated around the dining table after a special dinner on the evening of the exact day. There's a cake and ice cream and snacks and drinks; the celebrant receives presents; and the rest of the family sings "Happy Birthday." Sometimes Jacob is present and takes pictures, and sometimes he is not. The birthday celebrant is taken to the photo studio on a convenient day close to the birthday to have a special birthday portrait.

Occasionally, there is a special birthday party when family, friends, and neighbors are invited, and some have been recorded. For her sixteenth birthday, Angeline is having a big party the Saturday following her birthday. On December 18, the celebration will be as described normally. Then on the Saturday, she will have her birthday portraits, and there will be the big celebration with extended family and all the friends she wishes to invite (of course Angeline just has a normal group of friends). Angeline and her close friends will prepare lots of fruit punch, and Susan will buy soft drinks and have the food catered and pay for the DJ, which Angeline chooses. There will be food and music and dancing.

The birthday is celebrated, and Christmas is celebrated. Stephen has completed extra lessons in social studies. And then it is the New Year. All is quiet until the Easter celebrations.

Easter is celebrated much the same way as Christmas except that there are no lights and decorations, but the house is decked with the special curtains and bedspreads and cushions. The house gets a spring-cleaning, and the dining table is set on Holy Thursday. Easter bun and cheese are bought. Ginger beer and lemonade with brown sugar are made early in the same week. On Holy Thursday, a lot of fresh fish is eschovitch, and a large amount of macaroni pie is made to last for Good Friday and Holy Saturday. Susan and the children attend church services the evening of Holy Thursday, the morning of Good Friday, and in the night on Holy Saturday, which ends with the Easter Mass beginning at midnight. On Easter Sunday morning, they return from church at about one thirty. They eat snacks and go to sleep and awake late and have a late breakfast together.

During the Easter school holidays, after the Easter celebrations, Stephen's end-of-term test papers are reviewed, as is the custom, and he does all his corrections. Then he enjoys his school holidays. He likes to play in the neighborhood with his friends, playing baseball and basketball and having heated discussions. His older siblings, on the other hand, only have friends at school; during holidays, they meet their friends at the movies or at parties at the friends' homes.

Since they are in senior high school, the older siblings fully manage their own schoolwork. Susan only looks at their work out of interest in what they are learning in school. They are proud to show Susan their test papers, maybe because they are accustomed to doing so. The process is merely a sharing experience. They tell their mother what they think of the term's work. They share with her any difficulties they experienced with the subjects they like least, which now brings them some B's and B+'s on their reports. They talk about what caused them to make certain mistakes on their tests and how they will deal with their errors. And they teach Susan a thing or two that she may not have known.

The third term of the school year brings big finals for Angeline and Stephen. At the beginning of the term, Angeline sits her exams. Later in May, Stephen sits his final primary school examinations. The whole family waits anxiously to see what his results will be. It is taken for granted that Angeline will pass all her subjects and will graduate, but there is nothing like having the official results of Angeline's name appearing on the graduation list and Stephen's name listed among the students of the top academic group for high school. Stephen gets a B for social studies and A's for language and mathematics. Thus, his score is AAB.

During the third term also, Nicholas participates in a science Fair in the fourth form. His exhibit wins first place; he is credited for the most comprehensive presentation of his project. The first prize is a trip to another Caribbean island, where he will display and explain his project at a science exhibition and tour several historic and pleasure sites. His name is in the local news on radio and in the newspapers. He is very proud and excited, and the family is proud of him.

Angeline and Stephen are also happy with their results, and the parents are proud of all the children. Another academic year ends.

In addition to the usual excellence, a major milestone occurs. Angeline graduates from high school and is the valedictorian of her class.

Since exams were finished, the school band has been practicing every day and on Saturday mornings for the graduation exercise. So Angeline and Nicholas have been very busy. The band will also go on a performing tour of two neighboring islands during the summer holidays, and Angeline and Nicholas are included in the group as members of the band. When the older siblings are gone, Stephen will get the usual "before entering high school talk."

The day arrives for Angeline's graduation. She looks brilliant in her cap and gown as she, as the valedictorian, leads the graduation procession into the auditorium.

Susan looks stunning. Her hairdresser has done an excellent job, as usual, with her hair and makeup. Susan is always pleased with the way her hairdresser knows how to style her hair to suite her face and the way she applies her makeup lightly. Added to Susan's beauty, it creates a picture of utter glamor. Susan's dress is navy blue with a pleated skirt that reaches to her calves. The bodice is plain with straps on the shoulders. Over the bodice is a floral jacket with long sleeves and fitted at the waistline, held together with one button at the waist. The entire outline of the jacket is finished with a golden cord.

The hem of the jacket reaches her hips, which just accentuates her perfect figure. She wears navy shoes and carries a navy purse and wears gold earrings and a gold chain around her neck. Susan was very pleased when she looked in the mirror at home; now she feels quite elegant and confident. She is seated in one of the seats of honor provided for the parents of the valedictorian. The seat beside her, intended for Jacob, is empty, as he arrives late and takes a seat in the back. She is entertaining two emotions—one of pride and joy and another of utter loneliness and embarrassment, as the entire community witnesses the empty seat beside her.

Eventually, Angeline delivers the valedictory address. At the end of the speech, the entire graduating class responds with a standing ovation and cheers for their valedictorian. Shortly afterward, the ceremony ends, and Angeline does manage to get some professional pictures of the family with her father in them.

The outpouring of congratulations to the Wells family is enormous. People congratulate Angeline, as well as Nicholas and Stephen for their various accomplishments. They congratulate Jacob and Susan also. When Jacob receives congratulations he responds with, "It's their mother who trains them."

On arriving home, Susan finds a note on her bed that reads, "You look absolutely gorgeous today. Can I share your bed with you tonight? Your loving husband."

Well, Susan isn't even sure who the note is from, as she is not aware of having a loving husband. She is surprised that Jacob has found the time to come home and leave again in the time it takes her and the children to arrive home from the graduation. She wishes she didn't have to undress so soon, so she waits to undress after Angeline leaves for her graduation ball.

Angeline resembles her father. She is five foot seven with black hair that flows to her shoulder blades like her mother's. She has serious eyes like her father and his slender nose. She has soft, warm lips; a rounded chin; and a light brown complexion. Her shoulders are raised like her mother's, and her gait is confident. Now she is dressed in her graduation outfit and looks absolutely beautiful.

Her dress is made of forest green chiffon over forest green satin. It flows elegantly to her ankles from under the bustline. In front, the bodice is covered with sequins, while the back is closed with small buttons and loops. It is held on the shoulders by thin straps, and it has a forest green chiffon shawl. She accentuates the outfit with silver shoes and purse and silver jewelry.

Her prom date arrives just as her father does. After her father kisses her on the cheek and tells her she looks beautiful, her date puts a corsage onto her left wrist. Her father takes some pictures. Then she leaves with her date and his father and many wishes to enjoy her graduation prom.

At this point, Jacob acknowledges the note on the bed. Susan declines politely, explaining that the situation is too grave with the AIDS epidemic and that he has not built an emotional bond with her. She explains how embarrassed she felt sitting alone at the graduation and how lonely she felt then and feels at all other times. He invites her and the boys out for drinks, and they leave for the city. When they return home he spends the rest of the night watching television and then goes to sleep in the guest room.

For the entire next week, Angeline's voice is heard on the radio as the news of the graduation and the valedictory address is reported. A week after Angeline's graduation is Stephen's graduation, after which the family goes out to their favorite restaurant for dinner.

The summer holidays begin, and Angeline and Nicholas are away for two weeks on their school band tour. Stephen gets his 'before entering high school talk.' Susan tells him, as she told the others, "Now the teachers you will see come into your classroom have everything you will need and should want inside their head. Pay attention to them. They have been paid to come and impart to you everything that they know, and they are happy to do it. Watch them in their faces and pick up everything that comes from their mouths that pertains to the lessons. You pay attention to your friends when class is over. Another thing is that I do not go out of the house and embarrass you, and I would not like for you to go out and embarrass me. Going to school is your career until you graduate from high school. When you invest well in your school years, you make a foundation for yourself on which you can build and become anything you wish to be when you become an adult. Learning in school is something you do for yourself and not for anybody else. Make the most of high school. God's blessings be with you."

Nicholas and Angeline return safely, and the children spend the rest of the holidays at home occupying themselves with the many activities and games with which their father provides them in between meeting their friends at the movies and the usual going to the beach when Susan is off work. Stephen begins to anticipate and make plans for his winter trip to Canada.

The new academic year begins, and Angeline enters community college for an associate's degree in finance. Nicholas begins his final year of high school. And Stephen begins his first year of high school. All goes well for the Wells family, and the first term ends with the usual academic excellence.

It is time for Stephen to go to Canada for his experience of winter and snow. Everything is arranged for him to travel as an unaccompanied minor and be met in Toronto by his grandmother. Loaded with gifts for the Christmas party, he departs excitedly for his adventure. Susan and the two older children make the most of Christmas while they miss Stephen.

In no time, however, the New Year arrives, and Stephen returns with gifts for the family and some friends and stories to fill each ear and to entertain his friends when he returns to school.

The second school term begins, and Nicholas gets very serious about his final high school examinations. Stephen's first report is filled with A+'s. The months pass, and the family celebrates Easter, immediately after which Nicholas sits his final exams. Angeline also does exams for the end of her second semester in college.

Several weeks pass and Angeline and Nicholas's results are ready. Angeline has excelled in all her subjects, and Nicholas is graduating as salutatorian. He is very happy and the family is very proud of him. Stephen has only A+'s so far in his high school reports. He has done so up to this point without any studying at home. Nicholas is now busy with school band practice every day during the school hours and on Saturday mornings. The family is looking forward to the second major milestone—Nicholas' graduation from high school.

The day arrives and Nicholas looks academic because he wears glasses as he walks proudly beside the valedictorian, leading the graduating class to their seats. He delivers the salutatory address, in which he admonishes his classmates to be "outstanding role models wherever life may take you." The valedictorian is also male. In his address, he draws attention to the fact that, although most times it is a female leading in academic achievement, males are leading in this graduation. The audience gives them a standing ovation and a round of applause. Nicholas receives the special scholarship for salutatorians, which will finance his tertiary education. He plans to attend the local community college to obtain an associate's of science degree before moving on to university for his bachelor's of science degree.

Susan looks glamorous as usual. Her hairdresser has done the usual excellent job with her hair and makeup. She is dressed in light pink—a two-piece crochet skirt suit over silk lining. The skirt is long, falling to the calves, and the blouse is short-sleeved and reaches her hips. The blouse is pulled at the waist by a crochet string and closes in the back with a zipper. The hem of the skirt and blouse and the sleeves and neckline are all crochet finished. She accessorizes the suit with fuchsia shoes and purse and a black and white pearl necklace with matching earrings.

Although Jacob arrives late, he takes his place that is provided for the parents beside Susan, and Susan feels relieved that she doesn't have to experience the same embarrassment as the year before. Jacob wears a long-sleeved shirt with matching necktie and trousers. His color scheme is brown, and he wears brown shoes and socks. At the end of the ceremony Nicholas is able to have some professional photographs with the entire family and with friends.

Two hours later at home, Nicholas is dressed for his graduation ball. His father will chauffer him and his date to the ball, and Jacob is taking pictures of Nicholas. Nicholas is handsome and resembles his father. He has gentle eyes like his mother and a slender nose like his father. He is slightly taller than his father at five foot eleven and weighs 150 pounds. Tonight, he looks very elegant in a navy blue suit with white shirt. He wears a maroon necktie with thin oblique navy blue stripes and a maroon pocket square folded in the original style. He wears contact lenses now rather than glasses. One by one, the family embraces Nicholas and wishes him an enjoyable evening before he departs with his father, carrying in his left hand a corsage for his date.

The following week, Stephen's report is ready, and his grades are once more only A+'s. So for his entire first year in high school, he has earned only A+'s. Angeline gets a summer job with an accounting firm. Nicholas gets one with a travel agency. In their spare time, they go with their father to learn to drive.

Stephen spends one week of the summer holidays travelling overseas on a business trip with his father. When he returns, his end-of-year test papers are reviewed. After doing his corrections, he spends most of the rest of the summer holidays playing video games. He loves video games and is allowed to play real games on the computer like basketball and boxing. However, Susan has forbidden him to play those morbid fighting and killing games, and he has complied.

When the new academic year begins, Angeline enters her second year of community college, Nicholas begins his first year of community college, and Stephen begins his second year of high school. By the time the calendar year ends Angeline is eighteen, Nicholas is sixteen, and Stephen is thirteen.

A special birthday party is held for Nicholas, and he feels very pleased to be able to invite all his friends. Angeline helps him make fruit punch, and Susan caters more soft drinks and food and his choice of DJ so he can have dancing as well. The boys like to know that they receive the same privileges as Angeline.

The family celebrates Christmas in the usual way and Jacob visits whenever he wishes.

Chapter 13

STEPHEN IS DISTRAUGHT

Throughout the christmas season and into the New Year Stephen complains again about being sad because he has a broken family. He says it to his father, and his father just brushes him off with, "What you worrying about? You are not hungry, and you are not walking naked!"

Susan notes Jacob's ignorance and his callousness and feels sympathy for Stephen, who obviously has a different set of values than his father. It was Stephen who, in kindergarten, received certificates for being the most loving child in his class. He has also showed special loving qualities at home when, during afternoon rest, he would stand in the middle of the bed singing to his siblings. Susan hopes that he will grow up to be able to show love in giving of himself, where his father is evidently unable. She decides she will have to see to it that he goes on a trip during the summer.

At the beginning of 1999, Nicholas decides that, at the end of his first year, he does not wish to continue with community college. Rather, he wants to transfer his credits and go on to a specialized university to obtain his bachelor's degree in engineering. He gets accepted into the university that is his first choice and looks forward to having all his credits transferred.

Stephen's second year of high school comes to an end. In spite of his complaining and feeling sad, he manages to get another full year of A+'s on his reports, which he acquires without doing any visible studying at home. Nicholas completes his first year of community college and is successful in having all his credits accepted by his university. He will pursue a four-year program toward obtaining his bachelor's degree in engineering.

Angeline is graduating from community college with an associate's degree in business administration.

The day quickly arrives for her graduation. Once again, Angeline is leading her graduating class to their seats because she is the top student with the highest academic achievement. She walks very proudly and confidently in her ceremonial regalia. She has the responsibility and the honor of delivering the farewell address on behalf of her class. When, eventually, she gives her speech she pleases her classmates to the extent that they utter sounds of agreement and pleasure at many of the things she says and sometimes even interrupt her with applause. Susan and Jacob are not sitting with the other parents. Instead, they occupy special seats among the officially invited guests.

After the ceremony, Jacob takes the family out to dinner and takes pictures. On the following Saturday, he takes the children out to shop for clothes for their trips.

Angeline is not having a graduation ball this time. Her class has planned a one-week Caribbean boat cruise, which they will enjoy the first week in August. During that time, Susan and the boys will spend five days on the island of Sint Maarten and go to the beach there. Susan will take the month of August off on vacation, as during the last week in August, she will accompany Nicholas to his orientation.

Susan and the children have all returned from their trips. Susan is so happy that she had planned a vacation for the boys. Now Nicholas is going to leave home to go overseas, and she was happy to see how he and Stephen enjoyed each other's company on a one-on-one basis. She mostly, in her spare time, read a book or gathered cockles to make soup, while the two boys engaged in a good many activities together.

In the New Year, Angeline had decided that she did not want to transfer to university immediately after graduating from college.

Instead, she wanted to work for a year at her part-time job to gain more experience. So she worked during July, got a week off for her cruise, and then went back to work until the next summer.

At the end of the third week in August, Nicholas is leaving to attend university in the United States of America. Susan and Stephen leave with him to attend his orientation, at which they will spend seven days, leaving Friday and returning the next Thursday. Although Jacob had promised Nicholas to attend his orientation, when the time for departure was near he was not prepared. That's when Susan got the bright idea to take Stephen along, given how close he and his brother were on Sint Maarten.

Susan is happy to see exactly where Nicholas is going to live and attend classes and to meet some of the young people with whom he is going to associate. She observes Nicholas arrange for his classes and get settled in his dormitory.

When she returns home, she realizes the trip made the separation a little less painful. She hopes that the visit had the same effect on Stephen, who seems to have settled into high school for his third year.

Lo and behold, however, midway into the first term one Saturday when all seems quiet at home, Stephen says to her, "It is worse now than before. Now it is me alone living in a house with two women."

The only thing that appeases Stephen is to take a bubble bath every so often, and Susan tries to take him to the beach every Saturday morning. She tells him that Nicholas will be home soon for Christmas holidays.

Stephen only replies, "Then he'll be gone again."

Susan does not even bother to respond with, "And then he will return for summer vacation."

Her encouragement does not do any good, and Stephen refuses to be consoled. Instead, he sometimes cries on a school night and asks for his hands and fingers to be massaged for him to go to sleep. Susan is so taken up with him that she sometimes misses the news both on the radio and in the newspaper.

When she eventually catches up on reading some older newspapers, she learns that the country had just celebrated International Men's Day on November 19.

The Christmas season arrives, and Nicholas is at home for three weeks of holidays. Stephen is a little happier, as he spends quality time with his brother, and the two go together with Jacob to practice driving. Angeline got her driver's license in October and sometimes drives into town when she and Susan and Stephen go for work and school. Stephen is allowed to sit in the front passenger seat in an effort to make him not feel so much the effect of being a boy behind two women. It, however, never lessens his constant complaints about living in a house with two women.

The school term ends, and Stephen and Nicholas are at home while Susan and Angeline go to work until midday on Christmas Eve. By this time, all the food and drinks have been prepared for the holidays, and Nicholas and Stephen have decorated the house and garden with the Christmas lights.

Susan and the children observe their normal religious practices and Jacob visits on Christmas Eve night before they leave for church, bringing gifts as usual. They don't see Jacob for the rest of the Christmas season, which just reminds Stephen of his broken home and causes him to complain afresh about his sadness over the situation. The year 1999 ends on that note, with Angeline nineteen years old, Nicholas seventeen, and Stephen fourteen.

It is summer 2000, and another academic year ends. Nicholas has come home and is working at his summer job before high school closes for Stephen. In spite of his inner turmoil, which has taken him to a few tearful nights, Stephen has produced a year of A's and A+'s on his reports, and his father gives him a lot of money for his accomplishment.

Stephen refuses to put the money into his savings account. Instead, he buys many fancy sneakers. He also gets himself a holiday job in a restaurant very close to home and spends all his money on designer clothes and shoes. The people at the restaurant all love Stephen, and he works a full schedule during the summer holidays.

All three children are well loved at their jobs for their work ethics and their deportment and courtesy. Thus, they are allowed to work whenever they wish. They each also work from time to time when they did not intend to, when their supervisors need them, as long as work does not adversely affect their studies.

The summer ends, and Angeline is not ready to depart for university. She did not get her preparations done in time for the fall semester. She will, however, begin in the spring semester of 2001. She has had all her credits accepted at the university that was her first choice, and she will be able to complete her bachelor's degree in two and a half years. She and Nicholas will, therefore, graduate at the same time—the summer of 2003.

When Nicholas leaves this fall, Stephen is extremely sad. He refuses to be consoled by all of Susan's efforts. He does not settle down in form four. Rather, he starts the academic year in a very turbulent manner, often being late for school and causing Susan to be late for work. Susan refuses to leave him behind in the mornings, and that causes Angeline to take the bus sometimes. His teachers are reporting that he is often uncooperative and inattentive in class, and his test papers are way below his ability and his usual academic standard.

Susan understands his plight. Surprisingly, some of his teachers do also, as they suggest to Susan that he may be missing his brother.

Susan does not allow Stephen's turmoil to cause her to miss International Men's Day this year. As November begins, she is paying close attention to the news to find out how it will be celebrated this time around.

The news reports inform every one that this is the second consecutive celebration of International Men's Day and reminds the public of the way the country celebrated it the first year. The day was instituted by a gentleman in one of the larger Caribbean islands and celebrated for the first time on November 19, 1999. On Susan's island, it was celebrated nationwide with an exhibition in all the public libraries of the first black men to accomplish various achievements. On display were pictures and biographies of men like Jackie Robinson, member of the Hall of Fame for being the first black Major League Baseball player and whose number was no. 42. There was also Sidney Poitier, the first black person to win an Academy Award for Best Actor. Susan did not see the exhibition, which lasted only three weeks in the local library, but got her information form the reports in the local newspapers.

This year, however, the country is celebrating Outstanding Caribbean Men. The local celebrant is Robert Aldrin, simply because, within the past five months, he has been granted the status of Queen's Counsel. Susan reads what is said about each of the men on display. She notices that nothing is said of any of their families, and none of them has contributed to the advancement of young men in the Caribbean community—a demographic that is failing at such an alarming rate in the Caribbean schools, and later in Caribbean families. What annoys her the most is that, although Aldrin receives such an honor, he does not give anything in return by addressing the young men of the community about International Men's Day, or about manhood, which is something they are both lacking and seeking to understand and attain for themselves. Aldrin either hasn't noticed or doesn't care about the failing rate of boys in the local schools, or the lack of direction and purpose of many of the young men of the community, or the fact that so many boys are growing up without a father figure in their homes, to teach them how to be men. She wonders where all the other members of the local men's clubs are. None of their voices is heard talking to the community about the special day or encouraging young men in the ways of manhood.

Susan feels sure that, if a woman could do it for the boys, it would have already been done. But it is a man's job that only a man can do, and no woman substitute can suffice. She did not manage to get Stephen out to see the exhibition, and she does not think that there was anything of value to him. She decides that, when she goes to church the following Sunday, she will discuss these concerns with the priest and suggest to him that next International Men's Day, the church should be heard. She also decides to write a letter to the editor. She writes as follows:

Dear Madam:

I noted with deep sadness the way the community celebrated the second annual International Men's Day. It was rather strange that the usual leading male's voice was silent at this time and that none of the other men of the local men's clubs took the lead to promote manhood in the community. It seems to me that manhood for the leading male figures is something to be hidden from the light of day. Maybe the one voice was speaking for all when he said, "A man can plant his seed wherever he pleases as long as he turns back and waters it." Maybe, in that statement, the leading male role models had contributed to society all the morals they possess.

I wonder if anyone else but me noticed that, of all the "Outstanding Caribbean Men" on display at the local library, nothing was mentioned of their families. I would like to insist that a man cannot be successful, thus outstanding, until he is successful in both his roles as career personnel and as head of his home.

It seems strange to me that a person can be educated to one of the highest professional levels and enjoy as high a status as Queen's Counsel and display a low moral character. That is the reason I think that moral education should be taught in school. We cannot have leading male figures in the community trying to teach such low moral standards, as in the quotation above. What kind of society will we become? We already see the trend in the schools and on the streets. Do we or do we not wish to reverse this trend? And it becomes obvious that we will have to start with the young generation.

Yours truly,
Susan Wells

The end of 2000 arrives, and the birthdays and Christmas have been celebrated in the usual way. Angeline is twenty years old and has quit her part-time job in order to start university in the New Year. Nicholas is eighteen and has completed his first semester of his second year in university. Stephen is fifteen and is depressed and unstable; he has completed his first term in form four, with low grades on his report. Susan expected that, having spent Christmas with his brother, Stephen would be somewhat appeased. Instead, he is unhappier as he anticipates Nicholas's imminent departure.

Although Jacob promised Angeline he would attend her orientation, just as with Nicholas, he did not prepare himself to travel. So Susan leaves with Angeline the first week in January to spend six days, departing Tuesday and returning Sunday.

As soon as Susan returns, Nicholas leaves the Monday to attend university, while Stephen has already begun his second term in form four. Stephen does not feel like going to school. Many days he does not get out of bed to attend classes, and Susan has to leave him in the mornings in the care of the helper. He is, by the end of the term, an emotional wreck. Susan is patient with him, while she tries to show him that, because of his actual situation, he has an even greater need for his education so that he can soon become in charge of his own life and make it what he wants it to be. He is inconsolable and finishes the term poorly, with even more failing grades than the first term.

He returns to work at the restaurant during the Easter holidays and only seems a little consoled when he goes to work. His supervisor at the restaurant wants him to work on the weekends during school and occasionally a night or two during the week. He shows interest in that, and Susan allows him to do what makes him feel happy; she knows that he has the ability to master his lessons when he is feeling better.

However, he completes the year sad and depressed at home and troublesome at school. All his grades are low, he has failed several of his subjects, and he is dissatisfied with his own results.

His sister and brother return for summer. He seems a little happier as he works full-time at the restaurant, goes driving with his father and brother, and plays video games at home. Susan and the older children drive together daily into town and back on workdays. Both children are anxious to drive, now that Nicholas recently obtained his driver's license.

When the summer of 2001 ends and the new academic year begins, Stephen decides that he wishes to repeat form four. His father goes with him to school, and they arrange with the principal and guidance counselor for his repetition. He decides that his grieving is over. And when his brother and sister are graduating in two years, he wants to be also graduating, from high school. He continues working at the restaurant full-time during school holidays and part-time during the term; he does not have an extracurricular activity in school, and he enjoys what he is learning in the workplace, as well as his interactions with the staff. His coworkers treat him as a youngster and not as an adult employee.

STEPHEN IS DISTRAUGHT

The first term of the 2001 to 2002 academic year, the teachers are surprised to see Stephen's complete transformation. Susan is not very surprised. She contributes it to the fact that he was allowed to grieve and to acknowledge his sadness and to act out in his own way without any pressure to be what others think he should be and without any condemnation. On the other hand, his brother and sister are like a beacon in front of him. In addition, a poor year's academic performance is something he is not accustomed to and, thank God for his ambition, does not appreciate. Thus, he was left with only one logical decision, which he grasped. He decided to make a choice for betterment of himself—for his own well-being and prosperity. And Susan is happy for him.

At the end of the term, the planning committee for the celebration of Education Week asks Susan to write an article on "Homework" for a magazine it will publish for the occasion; Susan's children, the committee notes, always did their homework. Education Week is celebrated in the nation every second week in March, and there is usually an Education Week magazine. Susan agrees to write the article, and then school closes for the Christmas break.

Angeline and Nicholas come home for the holidays. They drive Susan to work and pick her up in the evenings so they have the car in the daytime to visit friends and go out with friends to lunch and to the beach.

Angeline has her twenty-first birthday in five days. She wishes to celebrate it with her friends on the Saturday following, with dinner at a restaurant and a discotheque afterward until dawn. Nicholas is nineteen, and Susan and Stephen sent him a care package in October at university. Stephen is sixteen. For his birthday, shortly after the term started, he did not wish for his gift to be money spent on a party, feeding and entertaining his friends and paying a DJ. He said some new sneakers were being released by Nike. He wanted to be gifted his birthday money to spend it on himself and acquire those sneakers. So between Jacob and Susan, they gave him six hundred dollars for his sixteenth birthday.

The past two years have been very emotionally charged for the Wells household. No one feels like he or she has the energy to do the usual Christmas decorations and take them down afterward. So the three children join together and put up a few lights in the garden and leave the house plain for relaxation. The children sleep a lot and spend much time in their individual rooms when they are not out with their friends. Susan just wants to read a novel during her week off from work. They must eat, so Susan prepares the food and drink with Carol's help.

Susan is surprised on Christmas Day when Jacob arrives to eat dinner with the family. The children had asked him to come, and he granted them their wish. Susan is happy for the family to sit down to a special meal in the home. Of course, she wishes it would continue, but she dares not set her hopes up high only to be disappointed. The family plays dominoes after dinner for about two hours and then has dessert of fruitcake with a drink of sorrel, after which Jacob leaves.

Susan observes Stephen's mood and notices he is a little gloomy on Boxing Day. But she is happy to see him make the effort to overcome his disappointment the day after.

During the Christmas break, Nicholas has the following conversation with Susan: "You know, I estimate that living off campus will be cheaper than living in campus housing. So I have arranged for a place with two other students in a trailer apartment. I want to buy a cheap secondhand car. Also, I will not come home next Christmas but will experience Christmas in another environment."

"Whatever you plan for next Christmas, do you think you can include Stephen in your plans?" Susan replies.

"Certainly," Nicholas replies. "He can certainly join my friends and me wherever we decide to go."

New Year's Day is spent quietly at home, and the children talk on the phone with their father, who sends greetings to Susan.

The following day, the children entertain a few friends at home, after which they turn their attention to returning to school and university. Angeline has completed one year of university, while Nicholas has completed two and a half. Stephen has completed four terms in form four. Angeline and Nicholas depart on different days and Jacob comes to the airport to see them off.

Stephen struggles with his sadness and overcomes, settling himself into his studies and filling his spare time with work at the restaurant.

In a short while Education Week rolls around in high school, and Susan's article on homework is printed in the magazine. It reads:

Homework: Parents Must Show an Interest
By Susan Wells

Parents have a duty to be interested in every aspect of their child's life, and homework is one aspect. Even if parents are unable to assist with homework, they should still show an interest.

Homework is a very important part of a child's lesson. It is the part where the child can master the material that was presented to him or her in the classroom. First the child follows and comprehends the lesson presented in class, but this is just the beginning. If the teacher sees fit, homework is given so that the child can practice the lesson. Later, the child studies to assimilate the lesson and again to recall and revise. Then the learning is complete. Students today need to understand that they must play an active role in the learning process. The teacher can only teach, but the child must learn. He or she must activate his or her mental powers. The parent needs to help the child to practice this during the homework period.

How does a child become active? If a child has difficulty with the homework, he or she must take measures to ensure its comprehension and completion. The child may do some research or investigation, revise the lesson of the day, ask a peer or an adult, or consult the teacher. All this must be done before the homework is due. This is where children of varying abilities will differ. Some will complete the homework in less time than others, but all will reach the same goal—that is, to understand the lesson.

Many children are failing in school because they persistently neglect to complete their homework. They offer a lame excuse that they do not understand. Yet they cannot say what they do not understand. Many of them return to class without reading the homework instructions. Parents are responsible for ensuring that children do their homework, and the responsibility does not end with saying, "Go and do your homework."

As stated earlier, parents must show an interest. They need to be curious about the homework and how it is done. This is mostly done when the child is young, because that is the training period.

However, adolescents welcome this kind of attention too. The habits the child develops early are the ones he or she will practice later.

"Delinquent children are products of delinquent parents."

"Delinquent children are products of delinquent parents, who often exhibit such characteristics in public. An example of this is the case of the disorderly and uncooperative parents" who gathered at the high school's gate on the first day of class to demonstrate their high level of indiscipline and to object to the principal's efforts to uphold the school rules. Two other examples are the number of parents who practice double standards and those who display low moral standards before their children. These behaviors affect children adversely. "Delinquent parents are, sometimes, products of a delinquent political, legal, moral, or social system."

"Delinquent parents are, sometimes, products of a delinquent political, legal, moral, or social system."

On the other hand, the following behaviors encourage children in a positive way. A parent should examine his or her child's books at least every weekend from the time the child begins school and starts to bring home books. Equally important aims are (1) to see that the child is taking good care of the books and (2) to observe the quality of work the child is producing. Firstly, is the work clean, tidy, and neatly organized? Secondly, is the work correctly done?

The parent does not have to know the subject matter to know if the work is right or wrong. The teacher puts a *checkmark* next to what is right and an *x* beside whatever is wrong. The parent can acknowledge and praise the child for the work that is correct. When something is wrong, he or she can question the child. What is wrong here? Why did you not understand this? Were you paying attention when the teacher was teaching the lesson? What is the correct answer? A diligent student will have a ready answer for the last question.

The parent must get answers from the child to all these questions. This becomes a discussion and a time of sharing. If the child has not corrected all of the wrong work, the parent must see to it that all corrections are done. There again, the parent may not know the right answers, but the corrections should be marked by the teacher. Any work that is still not understood should be explained by the teacher.

If the need arises, the parent should accompany the child to see the teacher. The parent can gain a wealth of knowledge and benefit from the child's schooling. Parents are told to spend quality time with their children, and this is one way to do so.

Can you begin to imagine the intellectual development of a child who is accustomed to this routine from day one? After the first year in school, the child will have developed a habit of doing all corrections, knowing all the right answers, and paying attention in class. After a short while, the child will bring all test papers and projects to show the parent. Why? Because the child knows that the parent is interested.

The parent's interest will stimulate the child's interest in the lessons. The child will want to have correctly done work to gain the approval of the parent and will also be interested in school. He or she will take pleasure in doing clean and tidy work and in doing homework. Parents have a duty to show that they are interested in their children's homework.

Many parents are happy and express their delight in the information and direction that they obtained from the article. One parent responded in the local newspaper and encouraged other parents to follow the direction of the article.

In no time, summer comes around. The two older children come home. All three of them work at their part-time jobs, and this year, all three work with their father in their spare time.

Although Stephen is living at home alone with Susan, she doesn't hear him complain about the absence of a male in the home.

Shortly after Angeline and Nicholas return to their respective universities, Nicholas outlines his plans for Christmas 2002, and Stephen starts making plans to spend the holidays with his brother.

Nicholas tells Susan that they are going to visit Las Vegas with friends. They'll spend Christmas Eve, Christmas Day, and Boxing Day in Las Vegas, and the rest of the Christmas break they will spend at his trailer apartment with his two roommates. By the middle of the semester, Angeline calls to say she has been invited by her American roommate to spend Christmas with her in Boston.

So Christmas comes, and Stephen goes to the United States of America to spend the holidays with Nicholas. Susan baked the fruitcakes early, and she mails one to Angeline and gives Stephen one to carry with him. She picked some sorrel and bagged them and sends them with Stephen with instructions to make the sorrel drink.

Instead of being alone on Christmas Day, Susan attends the Christmas morning Mass. After breakfast, she goes to volunteer at a homeless shelter that is serving a Christmas luncheon. After she and the children talk on the telephone Christmas night, she watches a movie and then goes to sleep.

The helper and her family come by to visit on Boxing Day because Carol knows that Susan is alone, and Susan goes out to dinner that evening with two friends.

For New Year, Susan goes to midnight Mass. She spends a quiet day at home, talking on the telephone to family in Canada, watching a movie, and going to sleep early.

Five days later, Stephen returns.

Chapter 14

STEPHEN OVERCOMES

It is June 6, 2003, and it is Angeline's graduation day. She is celebrating yet another major milestone in her life—graduating from university with a bachelor's degree in Science, in the discipline of business administration. The past twelve months went by so swiftly, with all three children working happily at their summer jobs after completing their next to last academic year. It was then that Nicholas announced that he was not going to graduate at the expected time, which was June 2003. Rather, he was going to graduate at the end of the following fall semester, December 2003, as he was working on something extra. He would not say what the extra was because, "It is to be a surprise."

It worked out well for everyone, as his and Angeline's graduations would have been the same day in two different states in the United States of America.

Stephen completed a very successful year his second time in form four and received a very good report. He has also just completed a very successful final year in form five and is graduating later in this same month—on June 20.

So once again, for the third time in six years, Angeline stands proudly in her graduation line. She is not the leader of the class, but she graduates with honors. The rest of the Wells family is there to celebrate with her. In honor of her accomplishment, when she returns home, the company where she has been doing summer jobs presents her with a bouquet of flowers and an offer for a permanent position.

On returning home also, Susan just catches the end of the news, which says that the keys for the new public hospital will not be handed over on June 16 as planned. The new hospital has been under construction since January 1996 and was to be completed in June 2001. In late November 2000, the announcement was made that there was not enough funds left to complete the project. There was much public discussion in the newspapers between various ministers of government and the contractors as to why the funds had been depleted before the completion of the project and who was at fault for not reporting the correct amount of money that would be needed for its completion. Under discussion too was a host of reasons, some financial, why the allotted time was not sufficient for the completion of the project. The resolution was to provide more funds and to extend the time to June 16, 2003. Now that June 2003 has arrived, the minister of health and the minister of finance and the contractors are all exchanging criticism and casting blame as to whose fault it is that the project is still not yet finalized. The contractors have said that they can complete the hospital by the end of the year, falling short of the original specifications.

All this makes Susan very angry. She knows what many people think the problem is, and she thinks the same thing as the majority of the population. Furthermore, the political discussions remind her of a very similar situation when a new high school was being built. The high school was never completed to specifications, and no one was held accountable. An entire block of classrooms and a laboratory were eliminated, and no one was made to account for the shortfall. She and many other ordinary citizens think that, in both instances, the funds have been mismanaged and that not all of the allotted financing has been put into the projects.

She decides to bring this to the attention of the politicians and to make an appeal to the government to manage the people's money wisely. In a letter to the editor of her favorite newspaper, she writes:

Dear Madam,

What has happened with the new hospital project is similar to what happened with the project for the new high school several years ago and maybe even with other projects that have slipped my attention. There is nothing unique about these happenings. It is the very kind of proceedings that have happened in several developing countries, which has led these countries into poverty and destitution. Poverty and destitution is where our country is heading if a stop is not put to such happenings right away.

Here is how it progresses. The country is a nation with substantial financial means because, if I read correctly, the country decided to finance the project itself. The plan is made and finalized, and a contract is given. The plan begins to be implemented, but is never completed to specification. Politics set in, and after much discourse and futile explanations and blame casting and self-acquitting, no satisfactory conclusion is made. After a while, the matter is simply forgotten, until the process is repeated with yet another developmental project. Eventually the nation's funds are depleted. The country is not properly developed structurally. Neither are the necessary social services developed. Thus, the country begins to borrow.

On the other hand, the people become sick and tired of the politics. They feel sure that they know what is happening to the public funds, but they cannot prove it. Most are afraid to say what they think. Taxes begin to rise at an overwhelming rate for the poorer class, until frustration sets in and violence is born. By this time, the country is overextended in debt, the infrastructure is in disrepair, and the common people are struggling to merely survive while they watch a selected few splurge and prosper. And widespread violence gets out of control. This is the destitution that can be seen in some of our neighbors.

Is that the same direction our country wishes for ourselves? Or does greed blind the eyes? We should strive to build a nation where all people have an opportunity to live and not one where a selected few can overindulge while the majority must struggle just to try to survive.

Let us not curse and criticize our elected officials, since doing so does not bring about any good. On the other hand, let us pray that those we elect and entrust with our welfare will be strong enough and inspired enough to overcome the temptations of greed and selfishness, which is so common to man. We, therefore, ask that now and henceforth, all projects and contractors are properly supervised and managed by our elected officials, to whom we give this job so that a stop can be put to the pilfering we very strongly believe takes place. And let us all work for a nation wherein all who belong will be able to prosper by means of a good education and hard work.

Here I wish to encourage the people to speak up. Open your mouths and tell your politicians what you expect. You employed them when you marked your "X" on the ballot. This will help to heal the anger that you feel when you hear and read the politics that they present, and it will prevent you from becoming frustrated and violent.

I could write a whole commentary on this, but I hope these few words will be taken seriously, and the good of our nation will be held high on the agenda.

Yours sincerely,
Susan Wells

June 16 passes with nothing said of the hospital.

June 20 comes, and Stephen stands tall and proud in his graduation line. The family is proud of him. Susan is more than proud. She is relieved of her anxiety over whether or not he was going to graduate, even though the teachers told her that they expected him to graduate. Susan never saw Stephen studying at home. He worked part-time at the restaurant all through his final four terms, except during final examinations. Now he wears a sash over his gown that says "Honors" and also a broad smile on his face.

Jacob and Susan sit with the other parents of the graduates. Susan looks her usual beautiful and elegant self. Her hair and makeup are done excellently. She wears a floral dress of autumn leaves on a royal blue background. The dress is a six-gored, A-line fit that flows wide to midcalf. It is complemented with a long-sleeved, royal blue jacket that is waist length with a low-cut Peter Pan collar and closes down the front with small royal blue fabric-covered buttons and loops. Susan complements the suit with light orange shoes and a purse to match the outstanding leaves on the dress. She wears gold jewelry to match with her wedding and engagement rings.

Stephen, along with the other members of his class graduating with honors, receives a scholarship, but it is smaller than those of his brother and sister and will have to be supplemented to cover his university education. His father promises him to pay his university expenses. Angeline and Nicholas are home for Stephen's graduation, and the family is able to have some professional portraits after the ceremony.

About two hours later at home, Stephen is ready for his graduation ball. He looks a lot like his mother and her side of the family. He is six foot one with wavy dark hair and a dark brown complexion. He has soft, loving eyes and a straight nose more like his father's with a rounded chin and weighs 155 pounds. He stands tall and confident with raised, squared shoulders. He is less quiet and more outgoing than his brother. Tonight he stands elegantly in a dark gray pin-striped suit with a light blue shirt and ocean blue necktie and pocket square. The pocket square is folded in a flamboyant fashion. Jacob, who is there to drive Stephen to pick up his date for the ball, takes pictures of Stephen. After hugs and kisses from the ladies and collecting his corsage for his date, Stephen leaves with his father. Susan, Angeline, and Nicholas go out in the city for a drink.

While Angeline accepts the full-time job offer from the company she has been working for during summers, the boys work in their usual summer jobs and work with their father in the evenings.

After the summer, Stephen enters community college to pursue studies for his associate's of science degree in business management. Nicholas returns to his university to complete his bachelor's of science degree.

The fall semester ends, and Nicholas graduates with two degrees. That is the big surprise. He receives a bachelor's of science in engineering, along with an associate's degree in business management.

All three children have equipped themselves with studies in business management and administration so they can be ready if their father asks them to help him in his businesses.

Two days after Nicholas's graduation on December 13, the Wells family returns to their home in the Caribbean in time for Angeline's birthday on December 18. Angeline celebrates with her friends and coworkers in the evening immediately after work and into the night. Susan rents for her a recreation hall, where she caters a buffet dinner and dancing until 1 a.m. There is no ice cream and cake celebration around the dining table for her, although Susan did buy her a beautifully decorated birthday cake.

The boys, however, each celebrated an important birthday. On September 28, Stephen celebrated his eighteenth birthday, while on October 21, Nicholas celebrated his twenty-first birthday. Nicholas celebrated with his friends at university. The family sent him, by courier, a birthday present and a fruitcake. Stephen celebrated small at home around the dining table. Once again, he asked for the money that would have been spent on a party to spend on himself.

Susan will talk from now onward about the young adults or the youngsters. There are no more children in the Wells family. It is a family of adults.

Susan and her youngsters celebrate a very lively Christmas season with all the decorations and meals and holiday traditions. Once again, Nicholas informs her that he will not come home next Christmas. He invites her to come to Arizona, her and Angeline and Stephen, and he will take everyone to Las Vegas for Christmas 2004, when he and Stephen will experience a Las Vegas Christmas for the second time. Subsequent years, he will experience Christmas in other foreign lands. Meanwhile, his plan is to return to Arizona in the New Year and find a job near his university and a one-bedroom apartment. There, he will live and work and save and prepare for studies leading up to his master's of science in civil engineering.

In the New Year, Stephen also informs Susan that he does not wish to remain a second year in community college. Instead, he will get his credits forwarded to the same university where Nicholas studied to pursue his studies for a bachelor's of science in business management. He says that will shorten his time living in a home with two women.

It is in 2004 that Susan is inspired by happenings in the community to write another commentary. She writes the following, which is published in the usual newspaper in the month of March:

Deliverance, Please, Lord
By Susan Wells

In picking up from where we left off in the 1980s, I told you wives that the answers to your problems were in the Holy Bible. Some of you either didn't believe me or didn't care enough to find the time to seek (see Matthew 7:7). I don't know what some of you have been doing at home or why I still see so many of the young men on the corners looking utterly aimless and unkempt. It tells me that the so-called leading men of our community have not yet redeemed themselves. Obviously, they do not possess the caliber. We *must* hear the voices! The correct voices must enter into the ears of these precious young men.

It would be good for them to also see a good example to follow. Instead, they are employed as hit men, murderers, and whatever else I may not know about. May the Almighty and All Powerful God raise His hand in their deliverance. And if some of these hit men and murderers and henchmen are from outside, they will have to go; I would advise them to go quickly because, in these last days, God is only doing a quick work.

On the other hand, may He bring His hand down mightily and weed out any leaders of our community who may be using the people's money for their own personal purposes and to do evil in His sight. Further, may God let all politicians everywhere know and understand that, when the people mark their X's, they are employing the politicians to serve their country. Still further, may He make them repay every cent while He demonstrates real might and real power and His justice in our land.

I would advise you unsuccessful parents not to spend your time looking at other families that have managed to produce ambitious and successful offspring. Instead, get to work and clean up your act. Stop being led astray for two dollars here and five dollars there. That is exactly how some of the political parties have managed to destroy several of the countries around us—when citizens were willing to be led astray for some small change into their pockets.

Please know that I am willing to share with you my own secret. When I found myself alone with my set of small children I turned to the Holy Bible for answers, and I received more than I looked for (Ephesians 3:20). I received support and comfort, as well as innovative ideas to care for myself and my children. I called on the name of God, and Jesus came. He and I raised those children, Jesus being the light and me on my knees with my Bible open. Oh! Glory to God!

I would like to thank the government for the foundation of education it provides, by which my children benefitted in those crucial times. I would also like to congratulate the government on the further progressive steps now being taken to provide as much education as possible in our small nation. This will ensure that our children do not have to leave home at too young an age but will be able to mature enough to face and conquer the many evils that await them outside. Teach your children the Word because the Lord delivers from every evil work (2 Timothy 4:18).

I tried to tell you ladies that marriage is a precious gift from God. It is a noble and beautiful state that a great many, if not all, aspire to. There are, however, some floozies who wear themselves out when they are young. When marrying time comes around, they are not marrying material. Thus, they try to attach themselves to your husbands. The Bible tells you all about the floozies that hunt for your husband (Proverbs 6:26). And the Bible also tells you what would become of those floozies (Proverbs 5:3–5). I spelt it out for you in 1988. Maybe if you pray hard enough, the newspapers will give you a review. Basically, though, only the marriage bed is undefiled (Hebrews 13:4). Therefore, the wife is sanctified, and she is a covering for her children. When I was young, they called all the others, the floozies, mattresses—just plain mattresses.

Now the analogy is that a mattress gets used and worn out and old and frequently has to be thrown out and replaced with a new one. That is why men with the condition have to keep jumping from one mattress to the next. It is a spiritual condition. If you read your Bible, you will find out. But Jesus told His disciples how some of these conditions can be broken (Matthew 17:14–21). So here I am spelling it out plainly for you wives who are already suffering and for you young ones who would like to avoid such suffering.

May God bless our country. May he bind all filthy hands and send all children of the evil one to meet their father where he is waiting for them. Hallelujah to the Lamb of God!

In this same year in June, Stephen successfully completes his first year of community college and is fortunate to have all of his credits transferred so he will complete his bachelor's of science in business management in three years. He spends summer working for the last time at the restaurant and preparing to move to Arizona. The middle of August, he makes the move and enters university at the end of August to pursue studies for his bachelor's of science degree in business management. Since he is with Nicholas and she is going to see him at Christmas, Susan does not accompany him to orientation. She saves her vacation to use some of it in December.

December comes, and the Wells family will be spending Christmas at Nicholas's. The fruits for the fruitcake are soaking, and Susan will carry them with her and bake the cakes in Nicholas's apartment. She has the sorrel picked and bagged, and she will make the sorrel drink there also. Shortly after Angeline celebrates her twenty-fourth birthday, she and Susan leave for Arizona to celebrate Christmas in the United States of America. The day after their arrival, Susan makes the cakes and the sorrel drink because, in another two days on Christmas Eve, all four of them will leave for Las Vegas to spend three days.

On their return from Las Vegas, they enjoy the rest of the week together. Susan and Angeline return to the Caribbean on New Year's Day to go back to work the following day. So the year 2005 opens for the Wells with Angeline twenty-four years old, Nicholas twenty-two years old, and both of them working and saving for university to pursue their master's of science degrees. Stephen is nineteen years old and just beginning his second semester in university to complete the first of three years in his bachelor's of science degree program.

Chapter 15

A FAMILY OF ADULTS

It's 101 William Street—that is the address of the homeless shelter. That is where Susan met Cassie, Cassie Robertson. Cassie is the owner of the homeless shelter, where she serves lunch and supper to homeless people six days a week and is closed on Sundays. She also provides showering facilities and a place where the homeless can relax from ten o'clock in the morning until two o'clock in the afternoon. Lunch is served at noon, and the shelter closes at two o'clock and reopens at five in the evening to serve supper at six. That is the shelter at which Susan volunteered one Christmas Day. Now, with Angeline having moved to the United States of America and she, Susan, living alone, she volunteers from ten in the morning until two in the afternoon on Saturdays.

Cassie is a tall slim blond from Montreal, Canada. She is five foot ten and wears her hair short, cropped at the nape of her neck. She has a pleasant countenance. At age sixty-five, she is a rich widow who has migrated to the Caribbean. She owns a home in a residential neighborhood close to Everson Park where Susan lives. She also bought a piece of commercial property on William Street in the city, where she operates a supermarket and runs the homeless shelter. She has been living on Susan's island for the past seven years, but Susan only met her on Christmas Eve of 2002 when she stopped by to inquire about volunteering. Cassie has one son who is an aeronautical engineer working and living in South Carolina, United States. Raymond, Cassie's son, is thirty-five years old. He visits Cassie every Christmas for one week.

Angeline was accepted into a master's degree program at the same university where she obtained her bachelor's degree. She will study for her master's of science in business administration. She left home in July of 2005 to get herself settled in a one-bedroom apartment in time to start her studies in the fall semester. Nicholas also entered a master's degree program in fall semester 2005. Both he and Angeline are expected to graduate in 2007, the same year that Stephen is to graduate with his bachelor's of science degree.

Angeline has a part-time job while she studies full-time, whereas Nicholas works full-time and carries a lighter load of courses. Nicholas plans to take courses during the summer semesters of 2006 and 2007 in order to graduate in December 2007. Angeline and Stephen will graduate in summer 2007. Jacob is financing Stephen's university program as he promised, and he contributes financially to Nicholas and Angeline. Susan also contributes financially here and there when the youngsters ask. She and her youngsters are celebrating Christmas 2005 with Angeline in Angeline's apartment in Chicago.

Susan sent all three youngsters money in a birthday card for their birthdays on September 28, October 21, and December 18. Now it is time to travel to the United States of America for Christmas. She will find out what each one wants for Christmas and shop for their gifts in the United States. Meanwhile, she has the fruits soaking for the fruitcakes, the sorrel picked and bagged, and the ginger grated and sealed in a bottle for the sorrel drink and ginger beer, all to be made in Angeline's apartment. Susan and Nicholas take some vacation in December. The 20th of December, both arrive in Chicago two days after Angeline's birthday. Stephen is on school holidays and arrives with Nicholas. He and Nicholas decorate the apartment and put up a medium-sized Christmas tree, while Susan prepares the food, which include a turkey and ham, and drinks. Angeline goes to work and helps when she is not working.

Christmas Eve 2005 arrives, and the Wells family starts the traditional celebrations with midnight Mass. On Boxing Day, they all go to a band concert in the evening. They spend the rest of the week relaxing in the apartment and taking a tour of the city in between Angeline's work schedule. Nicholas and Stephen leave for Arizona on January 4, as Nicholas must return to work.

Susan spends four more days with Angeline. She and Angeline go to see a play when Angeline is not working and Susan is not relaxing and reading a novel in the apartment.

As soon as Susan returns home, she gets right back to volunteering at the shelter and attending her dancing with the dance group. With all the travelling to the several graduations and for Christmas, she has been irregular at dancing. Now, as she feels the need for exercise, she plans to resume her regularity.

It is now fall 2006. The birthdays come along, and Susan sends the youngsters birthday cards with money so that they can buy themselves things they need or want. Stephen turns twenty-one on September 28. For his twenty-first birthday, apart from card and money, Susan sends him a beautifully decorated birthday cake with twenty-one balloons, which she orders online to be delivered to Nicholas's apartment where Stephen lives.

It is now a year that Susan has been volunteering at the shelter. She and Cassie have become good friends. Cassie likes Susan very much and has invited her home several Sunday afternoons for tea. On other Sundays when Susan does not want to eat alone, Cassie has accepted her invitation to have lunch with her at home. Cassie's pleasures are red wine and casino gambling. With no casino on Susan's island, Cassie regularly plays the lottery. She even encouraged Susan to buy a ticket once, but Susan is no gambler. Plus, she does not like losing. So she has never developed the habit of playing the lottery.

Cassie wins money from time to time, even if it is two dollars. Once, she won ten thousand dollars. But she still could not convince

Susan to play. So she buys Susan a ticket every now and then, but Susan never wins anything.

The Christmas 2006 season arrives, and Susan is very busy in the office. A project she has been working on to be presented the first week in January met with some difficulties and delays and is taking a great deal of her attention throughout December. Nicholas also does not wish to travel for the Christmas holidays that year. He desires to do some extra studying and save some vacation time in order to travel to Hawaii next Christmas, 2007. Stephen, who has been driving frequently without a driver's license decides to use the break to prepare and obtain his license. With all that, Angeline decides to come home to the Caribbean.

Cassie takes a liking to Angeline and takes her for the daughter she never had. In the two weeks that Angeline has spent at home, Cassie has bought her several gifts, including a Christmas gift. One gift was a lottery ticket by which Angeline won $2,500, but Susan has never won anything.

Cassie still misses her husband, who passed away almost ten years ago in a car accident and who, according to Cassie, was a very loving and devoted husband. She does not wish to remarry. She just wishes for her son to get married and have a family so that she can have grandchildren, especially a granddaughter. Cassie is a happy and interesting companion, and even a young person like Angeline likes her.

Although Susan is so busy with the project, she finds time to attend two of the local Christmas pageants and musical concerts with Angeline. She and Angeline observe a traditional Christmas holiday season, during which she sends by mail a fruitcake and prepared sorrel for Nicholas and Stephen to have as close to traditional celebration as possible.

January 2007 arrives and Susan does her presentation, and then Angeline returns to Chicago.

This is the year when all the graduations are expected to occur. For that reason Susan, takes two weeks of vacation in June. In addition, she saves some vacation time for December and the next January, when she will attend Nicholas's graduation and visit Hawaii.

On June 9, the family attends Angeline's graduation in Chicago. She obtains her master's of science in business administration. Jacob and Susan arrive on separate days in Chicago, where they meet Nicholas and Stephen. Then the whole family travels back to Arizona for Stephen's graduation on June 17, when he receives his bachelor's of science in business management.

As usual, Jacob rushes back to the Caribbean. Susan and Angeline spend a few days with Nicholas and Stephen before Angeline returns to Chicago to her part-time job and Susan returns home.

Angeline will continue to work part-time until December, when Nicholas graduates. Stephen will find himself a summer job until August, when he will start full-time studies for his master's of science in business administration in the fall semester. He has arranged for his father to support him fully financially so that he can complete his master's degree quickly, after which he will return home and work with his father. Nicholas will continue his full-time job after graduation so that he can keep the apartment until Stephen graduates in 2009.

Now that the youngsters are older, they put less emphasis on celebrating their birthday annually. They enjoy when the family can meet for Christmas, but with their desire to see the world, they do not always wish to come home. They prefer for Susan to meet them for Christmas celebration in some foreign city. Susan continues to get them each a birthday card and put some money in it. She mails Stephen and Nicholas's birthday cards to Arizona and carries Angeline's with her when she goes to Nicholas's graduation.

Susan takes two weeks of vacation—one and a half weeks before Christmas and four days in January 2008. She arrives in Arizona with Jacob on December 15 for Nicholas's graduation the following day. On a cold, wet December day, Nicholas receives his master's of science in civil engineering. Jacob leaves on the seventeenth. Angeline turns twenty-seven on the eighteenth. And Susan and her youngsters depart the night of the twenty-third for Hawaii.

They take a red-eye flight and land in Honolulu at 7:40 a.m. on Christmas Eve. After a hearty Hawaiian breakfast, they rest in their hotel rooms until the early evening, when they attend a luau. They are able to attend Mass on Christmas Day in the Roman Catholic diocese of Honolulu and spend an interesting Christmas Day and Boxing Day before they move to the Island of Hawaii on December 27.

They occupy themselves on the Big Island for the next week, attending another luau and visiting the many recreation areas and historical parks and the Punalu'u Beach. On January 3, 2008, Nicholas and Stephen return to Arizona, while Susan returns with Angeline to Chicago before she returns to the Caribbean on January 5 for work the following day.

After Susan's departure, Angeline spends just enough time in Chicago to give up her part-time job, sell all her furniture, and end her lease on the apartment. In addition, she completes two six-month personal development courses she was studying, which the family did not know about. At the end of January, she completes a course in ballroom dancing and a course in the study of wines, for which she receives two certificates of completion. They were two intensive courses, and with them, she kept herself occupied when she was not working. She was inspired to know about wines by meeting Cassie and seeing Cassie's love of wine. She learned about an academy that offers a variety of intensive, six- month personal development courses and decided to fill her leisure time with something useful and self-improving.

At the end of three nights in a hotel, she had disposed of all her furniture and the apartment. She arrives home in the Caribbean on February 4 and resumes her permanent job the following Monday.

Within three months, she is steadily dating one of her closest boyfriends, with whom she spent some of her leisure time before she went off to study. Susan learns that the two kept in touch during her years overseas and that they are very serious about each other. Susan is happy that Angeline has a well-rounded lifestyle and has developed herself in all areas of her being. Susan starts to increase her savings and to prepare herself for the day that she will hear that Angeline is to be married.

Chapter 16

A MULTIMILLIONAIRE IS MADE

It is now summer 2008. Stephen is the only member of the Wells family with summer vacation. Susan and the two older youngsters all have permanent jobs. Susan and Angeline have to plan for vacation time next summer to attend Stephen's graduation. They all also miss the folk in Canada. The youngsters would like all of them together as a family to visit Canada at Christmas and join in the Christmas celebrations of the larger family. They remember the Christmases they spent in Canada individually and would love for the four of them to spend Christmas 2008 as part of the large family gathering. With that, Stephen gets himself a summer job in Arizona so he can save some money for the trip.

The birthdays come in the fall, and Susan sends the young men birthday cards with money. For Angeline she just buys her a nicely decorated birthday cake. Angeline and her boyfriend go out to dinner and do not have any dessert at the restaurant but come home and have cake and champagne. Susan joins them for a short while before she goes to bed.

The Wells (except Jacob of course) have arranged and planned for the four of them to celebrate Christmas in Toronto, Canada. All the working folk have secured whatever vacation days they need to visit Canada from December 22 to January 6. Susan and Nicholas only needed three days in December and five days in January, because their offices close the entire week between Christmas and New Year. Angeline's office does not close, so she had to secure two weeks of vacation. The young men, travelling from Arizona, meet Susan and Angeline, travelling from the Caribbean, in Dallas, Fort Worth. From there, they travel to Chicago, where they change plane before landing in Toronto at seven forty in the evening of December 22. All four of them have winter clothes now, Susan as a result of her travels.

Susan baked three large fruitcakes and one small one for Cassie. She takes two large cakes to Canada and leaves one at home for herself and Angeline when they return. They are all accommodated in one of Susan's brother's home, the same home where the family will gather on Christmas Day.

At the gathering, someone is profound enough to take a head count. There are fifty-two persons gathered. The oldest is Susan's mother, the matriarch, at eighty-one years old. The youngest is one of the great-grandchildren, aged sixteen months. Visiting Susan's mother are seven children and four of their spouses, twenty-one grandchildren and two of their spouses, nine great-grandchildren, one younger sister, two nephews, one niece and her spouse, two grandnephews, and one grandniece. In the past, when the gathering was smaller, there was usually a professional group portrait. Now that the group is too large for one sitting, different groups get together and take nonprofessional photographs and share them with each other. The party is great fun for everyone at every age and is a success.

There is so much food at the end that everybody is invited back on Boxing Day for brunch. The second gathering is just as much fun as the first, although not everyone has returned. Apart from Susan's family, two of her brothers and their families also travelled from overseas to the celebration. This does not always happen. Sometimes, one or others of the overseas families do not attend. In order to entertain the families travelling from overseas, different homes plan cocktail parties in the evenings throughout the week leading up to New Year so that the guest families can spend as much time as possible with family they have not seen in a long time and will not see again for a while. The three guest families sponsor a buffet luncheon on New Year's Day in a restaurant to say thank you and goodbye.

After New Year's Day, the visiting families do a little bit of sightseeing, revisiting some of the interesting places they already know and having lunch on top of the CN Tower. Finally, January 6, 2009, arrives, and Susan and her youngsters are the last to leave. They travel together to Chicago before they separate; from there, the young men return to Arizona, while the ladies return to the Caribbean.

Before summer 2009 arrives, Nicholas pays a four-day visit home to the Caribbean to see if the government has an opening for him to obtain a job as an engineer in the Ministry of Communications and Works. The ministry offers him a job, which he accepts. He returns to Arizona and begins making plans to return home.

Finally June arrives, and once again the Wells family gathers in Arizona for a graduation. On June 12, Stephen graduates with his master's of science in business administration. The family visits the Grand Canyon by air before Jacob, Susan, and Angeline return to the Caribbean on June 15. By June 30, Nicholas and Stephen have gotten rid of their furniture and apartment and return home. Their Everson Park home is filled again with residents. Nicholas assumes his job with government, and Stephen goes to work with his father.

Two and a half months pass swiftly by, and it is the second Saturday in September 2009. Susan has a mind not to go volunteering. It has been raining steadily since Friday evening, and everywhere is very wet. Susan lies in bed for a while enjoying the rain, but at nine o'clock she decides that, even during rain, people get hungry. So she gets out of bed, gets dressed, and has a light breakfast of toast with butter and hot chocolate. She leaves home for the homeless shelter.

When she gets there, Cassie greets her with a lottery ticket and the words, "Here. This is for coming out in the rain." Susan is the only volunteer who turns up. Cassie explains, "I bought this ticket for you yesterday, and I was fearful that you were not coming out to get it. I was fearful that you would stay home because of the rain. I am very happy to see you, and I hope your ticket is a winner."

Susan takes the ticket and sticks it into her purse before getting busy with Cassie preparing lunch.

On Sunday afternoon, Cassie joins Susan and the youngsters for afternoon dinner. The menu is curried goat and fried chicken, rice with red beans cooked in coconut milk, fried plantains, fried eggplant, and a tossed salad. For drinks, there is lemonade and ginger beer, and for dessert, apple pie. The youngsters are so fascinated with Cassie and her stories of when she lived in Montreal that they have left Susan to prepare and serve dinner alone. They have been sitting around drinking wine and ginger beer and eating peanuts. Now Susan calls them to the table, which she had already half set since Saturday night.

Halfway through dinner Cassie asks, "Susan, have you checked your ticket to see if you have won something?"

"Oh, no!" Susan replies. "I forgot all about it in my purse."

"You know," Cassie explains to the children, "I bought a lottery ticket for your mother, and she hasn't even checked to see if she has won something."

At the end of dinner, when everybody is seated on the porch sipping his or her favorite beverage and chatting, Nicholas gets the ticket from Susan and goes to check it on the computer. After a short while, he returns looking shocked. He simply stands there, staring at everyone and saying nothing.

Everyone stares back at him waiting, until Cassie asks him, "What did she win?"

"The jackpot!" says Nicholas.

"The jackpot is twenty-five million dollars!" Cassie says. She gets to her feet and heads toward the computer.

Everyone except Susan follows her.

After ten minutes they all return saying, "It's true." "It's true." "We all checked it."

Susan goes with Nicholas with the ticket to see for herself and returns shocked and speechless. Another minute passes in silence as everyone just looks at Susan.

"Toward the end of the week I'll accompany you to the office to claim your winnings," Cassie says.

"What do you want me to do with the money?" Susan asks Cassie.

"Exactly what you wish to do with it," Cassie responds.

"I'll have to give you some of it," Susan says.

"No. Not a penny. I don't need any of it, and I don't want any of it. You just think clearly and make some wise investments," Cassie tells Susan.

"I'm going to buy you a lovely thank you gift, and I'm going to make some investments in my children and grandchildren. Then I'm going to invest in my retirement," says Susan. Then she looks at the children and says, "Consider yourselves debt free." She continues, "I am going to make a contribution to the church and two charitable organizations. One could be the homeless shelter if Cassie will accept it or else some other organization where they feed hungry people. One will be to a place that cares for sick children. When the money is deposited into my account, the first thing I am going to do is to say a prayer giving thanks to God and asking Him for wisdom in using it."

The end of the week comes, and it is a prominent piece of news that someone has won the grand prize, but no one has come forward to claim it. Cassie and Susan decide to wait a little longer.

Another week passes, at the end of which they go together to the office. Cassie has to show Susan the way to claim the winnings. In eight days, the money, less the applicable tax, is in Susan's account—some ten million dollars.

Susan decides to wait until the New Year, when she has fully overcome the shock of it all, to start spending the money. She decides to divert her attention to planning a Christmas party to attract the youngsters to celebrate Christmas with the family and to keep the family Christmas tradition alive, especially now that the children are going their separate ways.

The birthday season ends with Angeline's twenty-ninth birthday, which meets her living in her new home with her husband, Robert. Within the last twelve months, she has been engaged and married and moved from her Everson Park home. She and her husband plan to occupy her former room for the two holidays, Christmas Day and Boxing Day. Nicholas has invited his girlfriend to join the Wells family for the two holidays, and Stephen's girlfriend from Arizona is visiting for one week from Christmas Eve. With all the children paired off, Susan feels quite emotional and wishes that she and Jacob could reconcile and Jacob could move home to Everson Park.

It is Christmas Eve and the day for the party. Susan has invited Cassie and Cassie's son, Raymond, and others of her closest friends and some relatives. The youngsters have invited their close friends, and they have invited their father.

In the morning, on their way into the city for work (the young men and Susan are travelling together in Susan's car), Nicholas says, "Mommy, Stephen and I invited Daddy to the party, and he said he will come. We didn't think you would mind. Since the place is still open, we thought that, if he decided to come, he could be your date for the night."

"It is a wonder that he accepted your invitation," she replies. "But I would like for everyone not to mention my having won the lottery at the party. Let's just forget about it until after New Year's."

Carol, the helper, helped to prepare for the party. She has been invited, along with her entire family. This includes her two children, who are in their teens.

"It is okay for the children to bring a friend if they wish," Susan told Carol.

At the party, Susan finds time to dance with Jacob and to talk with him.

"Wouldn't you like to move back home and live a decent life and create a decent home base for the children now that they are going their separate ways and we are expected to soon have grandchildren?" she asks him.

"That is my ultimate goal. I'd be happy if you are open to it," he responds.

"Well, what did I do to you that has caused you to treat me the way you have?" she asks him.

"Not a single thing," he replies.

"So what obligations do you have out there that are keeping you?" she continues.

"It's best if you leave that alone," he replies, and the music ends.

Instead of a new song beginning, there is silence. Everyone looks toward the DJ and sees Nicholas and Charmaine, his girlfriend, standing there.

"May I have your attention, everyone. I would like to introduce to you all the future Mrs. Nicholas Wells," Nicholas says, and continues, "I asked Charmaine to marry me, and she said yes. So we plan to wed next year. You will all be hearing more about the wedding when the time comes."

The announcement is responded to with a round of applause. Then Susan sees glasses of champagne (which Nicholas had arranged) being passed around. Everyone drinks (according to the DJ) to the happiness of Nicholas and his fiancée. Then the music starts again.

The party is a huge success. Approximately forty guests attend; these are the closest friends and relatives of the Wells family. After the last guests leave at four o'clock on Christmas morning, Susan and Carol put away all the leftover food and tidy up the kitchen. Jacob, Nicholas, and Stephen rearrange the dancing area, and the home is back to normal by four thirty. Carol and her family leave, and Susan and Jacob and six youngsters relax before they shower and change into church clothes and attend the seven o'clock Christmas morning Mass. They return home at eight thirty and get three hours sleep before Susan makes and serves the usual Christmas breakfast of ham and egg with buttered toast and eggnog. After breakfast, all eight of them open presents and then go to sleep for the rest of the day.

At about six o'clock in the evening, Susan wakes up and starts to prepare dinner. Most of the food is already cooked, as she had prepared plenty before the party and had served only about half of it. There is turkey and ham and rice with pigeon peas and plenty of ginger beer and sorrel. So she prepares some candied sweet potatoes and a vegetable salad. They will have the usual fruitcake and ice cream for dessert.

By six thirty, everybody except Jacob is awake. The others awaken Jacob at nearly seven o'clock when dinner is ready, and they all eat in the dining room. Susan makes sure to steer the conversation, ensuring it focuses on the children to avoid any of her children mentioning her lottery win.

"So you gave us quite a surprise, Nicholas, with the announcement of your engagement. When are you two thinking of getting married?" she says to Nicholas and Charmaine.

"Next June," Charmaine says.

Nicholas adds, "Charmaine has always dreamed of being a June bride, and I think we can pull it off."

"How did you and Jennifer meet and how long have you known each other?" Susan asks Stephen.

"We met last year on Valentine's Day at a party on the university campus—not this year's Valentine's Day but the one before," Stephen replies. "And we have something in common. She loves to play video games just as much as I do. We spend a lot of our spare time playing together."

"Sometimes I win too," adds Jennifer.

"How did you learn to play so well?" asks Angeline. "Because Stephen plays very well."

"I have a twin brother with whom I am very close, and we play a lot. My other brother, who is six years younger than us, plays a lot too. I don't have a sister. So we all play together a lot."

"So if your and Stephen's relationship develops into marriage, we could be having twins in the family," notes Nicholas. Turning to Robert, he asks, "Do you happen to have any multiple births in your family, Robert?"

"No. And Angeline and I won't be having any kind of births in the near future."

"That's right," adds Angeline. "We are planning to wait two years before we start a family."

The conversation continues after dinner and dessert, over coffee in the living room. The eight of them discuss what sex child the youngsters desire to have first and how many of each sex child each couple would like to have. They talk, too, about the siblings and the families of the outsiders. Then after coffee, they watch a movie.

At bedtime, Jacob decides to spend another night at home and he goes to sleep in the bedroom with Susan. Charmaine and Jennifer occupy the guest room, and Nicholas and Stephen sleep in their own rooms.

They sleep until eight thirty next morning, when the last person, Jacob, wakes up. Susan and Angeline are already making breakfast, and they all eat within a half an hour. They enjoy the usual Boxing Day breakfast of ham and eggs with buttered toast and hot chocolate. Jacob leaves after breakfast to attend to his businesses.

The rest of the day is spent quietly at home. The younger people lounge around and get to know each other better. They play board games and video games and eat leftovers as they wish, while Susan takes a nap.

Susan wakes at four o'clock and talks with her family in Canada. Everybody just enjoys eating informally and playing games until eight o'clock in the evening, when Robert and Angeline leave for their home. Nicholas takes Charmaine home in the other car, and Stephen and Jennifer get ready to go out with Susan's car to enjoy the city by night.

Susan is surprised to see Jacob return in the night to sleep at home.

"How would you like it if I moved home in the New Year?" he asks Susan.

"You are free to do whatever you wish. You built this house, and it is supposed to be your home. I would like, however, to have a clear understanding of the terms and conditions under which you propose to live here. I would not wish for any conditions that will be stressful for me," she replies.

"What conditions do you propose?" he asks.

"It would have to be entirely different from the way it was before. You would have to want to live a normal, decent married life, showing me the kind of consideration and respect that is due to a wife. Therefore, you would need to know about such conditions and how to accomplish them. I don't know whether it is lack of knowledge or just careless ways that you display or if you had specific problems in the home that influenced your behavior and caused your eventual departure," she explains.

Jacob is silent.

Susan continues, "I would need you to occupy the guest room until I ascertain how serious you are about living a life that I would consider normal and decent; and I feel like you know what I am talking about."

"How long do you think this probation period should last?" he asks.

"I think about a year. I cannot afford to invest my emotions until I am convinced of your real intentions. I wish to see you strengthen your spiritual and emotional being and become a more responsible and upright person," she replies.

He asks, "Can I share your bed tonight?"

"Why?" asks Susan. "What is special about tonight?"

"You have always been special, and I never stopped loving you," he replies.

"You say things like that and cause me to be waiting all this time to see you prove them, but I will not make any hasty decision that could bring me harm and more pain. You can sleep in Angeline's room until Jennifer leaves on New Year's Eve. Then you can move into the guest room, and we will take it from there," Susan replies, although her entire being just wants to say yes and to embrace her husband.

After that conversation, Susan is not ready to sleep. So she turns on the television to watch a *Bonanza* show. Only she and Jacob are at home, and they watch the movie in silence. Then she goes to bed, leaving Jacob in the living room. Before she falls asleep, she hears Nicholas come home. He converses with his father in the living room.

When she wakes next morning, she does not see Jacob in the house, and she does not ask anyone for him.

During the week that ensues, Nicholas goes to work in the second car; he does not have the week off now that he is working with the government. Stephen uses Susan's car to go and come, taking Jennifer sightseeing, to the beach, and other places. Susan occupies herself at home. The situation with the cars is that Susan had a car all along. When all three youngsters returned to live at home, she helped them as they joined together and bought a second car; they all agreed with her that two cars were enough to serve the four of them. They called the purchase just that—the second car or the other car.

On New Year's Eve, Stephen takes Jennifer to the airport for a midmorning flight. In the evening, Robert and Angeline move into Angeline's room for the holiday next day. Nicholas and Stephen, Robert and Angeline, and Susan attend midnight Mass together and return at 1:30 a.m. and spend their traditional New Year's Day.

So the New Year meets Angeline twenty-nine years old, married, and living with her husband. Nicholas is twenty-seven years old, engaged, and preparing to be married in June 2010. At twenty-four years old, Stephen has a steady girlfriend and is thinking he has found that special someone. Susan, at fifty-eight years old, is a multimillionaire and making the best of what life has to offer her. Jacob, however, is the very same person he was in 1980 and has not improved himself in any way, not even toward being the head of his family and a leader in his own home.

Chapter 17

IS IT POSSIBLE TO SAVE THE MARRIAGE?

Susan has planned her life in a way that will keep her very occupied and involved with her children and grandchildren way into retirement. Carol will continue to work at her house so the large home will be kept clean, and Carol will be happy to keep her job. When the grandchildren come along and their parents return to work, the parents will bring the grandchildren to Susan's home in the mornings, where they will be cared for during the day. When there are three grandchildren, a cleaner will be employed to keep the house clean and give Carol time to care for the babies. While there are just one or two babies, Susan will continue to help with the laundry in order to give Carol enough time to take good care of them. Carol will cook for everybody, and the parents will come to Everson Park after work to have dinner and then collect their children. The youngsters have endorsed this plan, and everybody is happy with it.

During the first week in January, before the bank can calculate more interest and before another mortgage payment is due, Susan goes to the bank with Robert and Angeline and pays off their mortgage. The bank was expecting their visit because the young couple had already notified them of their intention to pay off the loan.

Next, Susan advises Nicholas and Stephen that, whenever they each find themselves a moderate home, she will help them to buy it in cash. She is only giving her children a head start in life, and she expects them to make the best of it. She estimates seventy-five thousand dollars for each grandchild when he or she is born, but she does not tell this to her children. However, she tells it to Cassie, who agrees with her.

"In fact," Cassie says, "I have a similar plan for my grandchildren. But I will not tell it to Raymond until the time comes."

One week passes and then two weeks pass in January, and Jacob does not move into the guest room. He stops coming by, and he does not call to say anything. Susan concludes that he is too proud to humble himself and admit to less than acceptable ways and to try to make changes. She is satisfied that she has put all her love and effort into her marriage and family so that, if her marriage ends, she does not feel responsible. It may have even ended a long time ago, and she has not accepted it. But she always felt that Jacob would come to his senses one day and have the desire for a more elevated lifestyle. She even thought that Jacob would one day become aware of his surroundings and have the desire for a better standard of living as is available in his matrimonial home. But none of this has happened in thirty-one years.

After all this time, Susan only now realizes that it is time for her to move on with her life. Unlike Cassie, she would love to remarry. But her heart is only now becoming free, as she is sure that Jacob has had all the opportunities to be her husband if he so desired.

On the third Sunday in January, Robert and Angeline are eating a late afternoon dinner at Everson Park, as they frequently do on Sundays. Just as the family is about to eat, Jacob visits and decides to eat with them. Susan does not try to ask him any question; she is not going to pressure him to come home and then have him hurt her all over again. With just family at the table, she can feel her youngsters, especially the young men, bursting to talk about her lottery winnings.

Eventually Nicholas says, "Mom, it is the New Year now, so we can talk about the lottery and tell Daddy about your good fortune."

"Yes, Daddy. You know that Mommy won the lottery recently. They have already paid her and she has all that money in an account," says Stephen.

"You mean the twenty-five million that has been in the news that they say no one has come forward to claim?" asks Jacob. Turning to Susan, he says, "So you are that lucky bastard. I would not have guessed."

Then Angeline interjects, "It could never have happened to a more deserving individual; to think that it's her charitable and unselfish spirit that has brought her this fortune. If she hadn't gone to volunteer, she would never have met Cassie, who bought her the ticket."

"And Cassie says it is because of her work ethics and sense of commitment that they became friends and that caused her to go out to volunteer on that rainy Saturday that she was able to receive the ticket," adds Nicholas.

"Who is Cassie?" Jacob asks.

"The woman I introduced you to at the party," replies Susan.

"I mean, who is she? What is she all about?"

"She owns the supermarket on William Street, and she operates the homeless shelter where Mommy volunteers," Angeline hastens to explain.

"Oh! I thought I had known her from somewhere! It's that supermarket. She does a good job with it. You can find anything you need in there," Jacob exclaims.

"She is a very good businesswoman, and she attracts wealth. She is very wealthy, and she usually buys Mommy lottery tickets when Mommy goes to volunteer," adds Angeline.

Jacob becomes silent and pensive. Susan hastily steers the conversation to Nicholas's wedding, since that is the next topic of interest in the family. She knows that Jacob is wondering how much money she is going to give to him or invest in his businesses. But Susan is not going to invest her money to the benefit of the likes of his women, who are happy to break up families and try to take another woman's husband for their own. She knows that she has not heard the last of Jacob; he is just waiting for when he considers the ideal time to ask her for money. And she knows what her response will be. The most she will consider is to give Jacob a small cash gift. But that will be when everything is over and he least expects it.

Susan feels very happy to know that she is financially set for retirement. After contributing to her three chosen charities and giving her mother and siblings a cash gift each, she gets advice from Angeline and a mentor of Angeline and makes a proper investment that will pay her monthly when she is retired, to supplement any pension that she might have. At the end of all this Susan realizes that she never thought further about Jacob. She has been so preoccupied that Jacob is fading from her mind and her heart.

Until—*r- r-r-r-i-n-g, r- r-r-r-i-n-g, r-r-r- r-i-n-g*. Two days before the month of January ends, Susan's telephone sounds, and she answers, "Hello."

"Hi, love. Congratulations on your great fortune. I had to make a sudden business trip overseas, and that is why you did not hear from me." Susan recognizes Jacob's voice on the other end of the line.

"Why, thank you. I hope your trip was successful," she responds.

"Can we meet over dinner and discuss a business proposal?" he asks.

"Twenty-six years you have been in business, and only now you wish to discuss a business proposal with me, your wife, Jacob?" she asks him.

"Well, nothing ever happens before the right time," he says.

"The right time for any kind of discussion to have started between you and me was 1979, when I was your newly wedded wife. And any business proposal to be discussed was to be 1984, when you started out in business. After the way you were dishonest and disrespectful to me, I would be a fool to think I could enter into any kind of business relationship with you. And of all the discussions and relationships I have tried to have with you over the years, I would be an idiot to think I could start one with you at this stage of my life. It was because of your irresponsible, unfaithful, and dishonest ways that I did not make any effort to be recognized in your businesses. I will not discuss any kind of proposal with you, Jacob," she retorts.

"I knew you were going to want to say things like that, but you should look at the bigger picture. Think of what expanding our businesses could mean to our children's future," he says.

"I have been thinking of that all these past twenty-six years and eventually had to write it off as a loss, just as I have written you off as a loss, Jacob. The children and I don't know who your businesses belong to, and I would not invest my money to the benefit of your kind of associates. You are wasting your time and mine if you try to continue this conversation," she says.

"We can still have dinner for love's sake. You know I have never stopped loving you," he tells her.

"I had loved you too, Jacob. But love was never enough for you, and you have never told me what the problem was. It's too late for anything to start between us now that God has blessed my future and that of our children and grandchildren. I wish you every blessing in life and also in the afterlife," she tells him.

"Think carefully about an opportunity you will be missing. And when you change your mind, you know where to reach me. I won't give up on you, love. Take care of yourself," he says.

"You do the same. Goodbye, Jacob," she tells him.

Her heart feels light and free, and she actually feels happy that she had that conversation with him, which serves as a final closure to their acquaintance. She is happy for the way it ended with goodbye, and she has no intention of entertaining any such long conversation with Jacob again. He has proven that he has nothing healthy to offer her, and any further communication he wishes should be through their lawyers.

CONCLUSION:
THINGS I WISH MY BOOK TO DO

1. Teach mothers that, even if the father has abandoned his unique role in the family, it does not mean that the children should be abandoned.
2. Show young people that, with an education as their foundation, they are equipped to navigate their life successfully in spite of problems, which are normal. Thus, they should get their education before they get involved in adult affairs.
3. Show governments of developing nations that they should cease from blindly following "developed countries" but should think clearly of the conditions they want for their own nation.
4. Teach people that they should not look to other people for their well-being and happiness. Rather, they should look to their creator who made them and understands them. Atheists should look to their source of origin, strength, and power for their help.
5. Give enjoyment to the reader.
6. Cause people to change if they see themselves in any of the characters in the story and do not like what they see.
7. Teach parents and their children that children need not fail in school, except under some extreme adverse circumstances beyond their control. As soon as a pupil starts to struggle in a subject area, get help for the child.
8. Let everyone understand that teachers are trained and paid to teach. They report to school to impart their knowledge to the children in their classroom. All parents and their children should understand this and take steps to benefit fully from this service.
9. Let everyone understand that parents are responsible for their children's education, and education is not provided only inside a classroom.

ABOUT THE AUTHOR

Valerie Frett is a former educator of Caribbean descent. She spent her earlier years studying language and linguistics. In her spare time, she enjoyed reading about families, family relationships, and responsibilities. Mrs. Frett is a parent of three. Applying some of the insights gathered from her reading, she was able to equip her children with strong family values. In *The Making of the Family*, she would like to share some of these insights with a wider audience. Mrs. Frett is also a former writer for her local newspaper.

www.ingramcontent.com/pod-product-compliance
Lightning Source LLC
LaVergne TN
LVHW041814060526
838201LV00046B/1264